JULIE HALPERN

THE

F

IT

LIST

For Liz

SQUARE FISH

FEIWEL AND FRIENDS · NEW YORK

SQUARE
FISH

An Imprint of Macmillan
175 Fifth Avenue
New York, NY 10010
macteenbooks.com

Square Fish books may be purchased for business or promotional use. For information on bulk
purchases, please contact the Macmillan Corporate and Premium Sales Department at
(800) 221-7945 x5442 or by e-mail at specialmarkets@macmillan.com.

Library of Congress Cataloging-in-Publication Data Available

ISBN 978-1-250-05695-5 (paperback) / ISBN 978-1-4668-4849-8 (e-book)

Originally published in the United States by Feiwel and Friends
First Square Fish Edition: 2015
Book designed by April Ward
Square Fish logo designed by Filomena Tuosto

10 9 8 7 6 5 4 3

LEXILE: 730L

For Liz and Allyx,
the world is a much better place with you in it

And for Tobin,
our house doesn't feel quite like home without you

CHAPTER

1

THE ONLY THING WORSE than having my best friend sleep with my boyfriend the night of my father's funeral would be if she killed my dad herself. Becca didn't, which was the one thing that redeemed her. Still, I allowed myself the entire summer after the trampful event to be mad at her.

It's not as though I haven't done shitty things to Becca. In third grade, I announced in front of our whole class that she would never make the lead in the school play because she had boy hair. Which she did. Kind of forward-thinking of her for a third grader, although it was probably her mom's choice after the Lice Crisis of Room 143. In junior high I managed to leak the fact that she stuffed her bra when a tuft of tissues fell out of her shirt, and I yelled down the hall, "Becca! I think one of your boobs fell out!" And just last year, even though I swore everyone already knew, I let slip that she lost her virginity to her second cousin the night of her Bat Mitzvah. All of the above seemed unforgivable at the times of occurrence, and yet she forgave me.

Just like I forgave her for stealing my thunder as Mary Todd Lincoln in the fourth-grade play by accepting the lead male role of Honest Abe. After that, the entire play went drag, and Becca was hailed the class comedian. I quickly learned I preferred being behind the scenes, anyway. I also forgave the time she announced I had my period in sixth grade by asking in front of the alpha girls if that's why I took so long in the bathroom. And the time freshman year when she accidentally shredded my twelve-page English essay because she thought they were pages of my pathetic attempt at a vampire novel she needed to rid the world of.

Best friends forgive each other. And I knew I'd forgive her for screwing Davis. Eventually. It's not like he was my one true love or anything. We had only gone out for a month before my dad was killed in a cab on his way home from the airport. Davis and I didn't talk until two days after the news of my dad went around. I had to call *him* to get some sympathy. Maybe if I'd had sex with him, he would have called sooner. But there was something about him that turned me off. He was always listening to misogynistic rap songs with ridiculous lyrics, like, "With my nuts on your tonsils."

"Sick." I reacted to the lyrics.

"What?" he asked incredulously. He was always incredulous.

"Dude, that's like me saying, 'With my ovaries on your uvula.'"

"Is my uvula near my johnson?"

It wasn't worth an answer. It was just one of those lazy boyfriend situations because I was bored while Becca was off starring in the school musical, and Davis was always around. Plus, he had a car. At first, his long, wavy hair and busted-up knuckles from working his dad's deck-sanding business were a turn-on. But the thought of his nuts on my tonsils? Not so much.

It's not like Becca slept with guys all the time, although losing her virginity to her second cousin at the ripe old age of thirteen made it sound like she did. He wasn't a blood relative; there were divorces and remarriages. And he was older and super hot, plus there was Manischewitz wine involved. It was stupid, she was mortified, and lucky for her the only consequence was the agonizing guilt and residual slut label that hung around for a couple of years. That wore off once we hit high school and other people really started sleeping around.

And it's not like Becca didn't give me a good reason for the sexual mishap with Davis. Becca loved my dad. I did, too, of course, but Becca had never had a real dad in her life, so she idolized mine. Her parents divorced when she was one, and all Becca knew from men were her mom's grotesque attempts at finding fatherly replacements. Becca preferred my dad, a constant and caring male authority figure. Since we were little, he sort of became my designated parent while Mom attempted to wrangle my younger twin brothers, AJ and CJ. (Our family likes to shorten names as much as possible, so Andrew Jacob and Charles Joshua became AJ and CJ, and I went from Alexandra Judith to Alex, occasionally Al.) Dad took me and Becca to parks, zoos, museums, and restaurants throughout our childhood. As we got older and the twins became more outdoorsy, Dad broke out the camping equipment and fishing poles. I preferred camping in front of the TV, but Dad was still the go-to parent for talks. Becca even somehow managed to share in my first big sex talk from Dad, which went something like this, "You go near a boy's penis, it better be wearing a condom." Dad was frank and realistic about things, which is where I got it. He wasn't afraid of his daughter going out and experiencing things. At least, he never showed it. Like when I told him I really wanted to study film when I head off to college, he didn't try to convince me to go into something more practical, like Mom.

"You're so good with numbers, Alex. You could be a math teacher. Or an accountant." Mom was sweet, but way serious about life. Dad always said life was too short to be serious.

I wish he wasn't right about that.

While I huddled with my mom and the twins at the funeral, Becca was in Davis's backseat drowning her sorrows between her legs.

She told me about it, which was *something*. When the funeral ended, and we went back to our house for shivah, Becca busted in the door bawling her eyes out. It wasn't beyond Becca to milk any situation for drama (she was well known for her crying-on-cue abilities), but this was over the top. She dragged me by my black-sleeved arm up the stairs of our house, so I grabbed for a tissue and thrust it at her. Instead of taking the tissue, she dove into me and cried between gulps and heaves, "I'm so sorry, Alex. So so sorry."

"I know. It's horrible. But you didn't kill him. Stop. You're crying more than I am."

That drove her into another crying jag that lasted a good five minutes, complete with hiccups. I was all cried out from hospital visits and coffin choosing, so I lay down on my bed and stared at the green-tinted, glow-in-the-dark stars on my ceiling. Becca, of course, helped me affix those back in sixth grade.

When she managed to calm herself and finally took advantage of the tissue, she whispered with a look of wide-eyed horror, "I slept with Davis."

I didn't say anything, unsure whether she meant they just took a nap together. Like, how the word "ridiculous" can be good or bad.

"In the back of his car," she continued, and the meaning cleared up.

"What? Why?" My empty stomach tensed into an even larger knot than had already rested there from my dad's death.

"I'm sorry, Alex, it just hurts so much, and I felt so alone because I'm not really part of your family and Davis drove me to the funeral and we smoked some pot in his car—"

"What?" Becca and I were anti, so that was a double "what?" One of our favorite party pastimes was insulting people who drank or smoked because they were too insecure to show their real selves. Unlike us, we thought superiorly.

"I didn't know what to do. He offered, and I thought it would make things feel not so bad, and then I just felt sleepy and he was so close and I was wearing a skirt with no tights because it was too hot—"

"TMI, Becca. Stop before he inserts his penis."

She laughed because it did sound absurd. But she wasn't allowed to laugh. She was my best friend. My dad just died. And she slept with my boyfriend. Who I had planned to break up with anyway, but still.

"I can't deal with this now." I stood up. "There are people down-stairs waiting for me."

"I'm really sorry." The tears tumbled out of her eyes again, but all I could do was give her an exhausted glare.

"Don't call me, okay? Don't text or email or smoke signal or anything. I need some space right now."

"Are you breaking up with me?" she choked.

"I just need us to take a break. I don't need something else to deal with." I stood up without another look at Becca and walked back downstairs to accept the trays of deli food and hugs of sympathy from everyone who knew and loved my dad.

That was the beginning of June and the end of our junior year. Becca called, texted, emailed, messaged, left notes in my mailbox, and sent a muffin basket. It was all duly noted in my mind, but I meant what I said. I needed some space and time to process the summer of shit I had ahead of me. Mourning the loss of my dad, helping my mom with two middle-school brothers, and working at Cellar Subs was all I could handle. I steered clear of social situations, unless they involved family, and I dove deeper into watching horror films as inspiration for a movie I planned to make someday.

The first day of senior year, the plan was to head straight to Becca's locker and tell her, "Okay, I'm over it." Then hug her and never look back.

Only it didn't happen that way. Because Jenna Brown, a peripheral friend who was fun because of her song-parody-writing abilities but also lame because of her obsession with weight loss, waited for me by my locker. When she saw me, she offered her arms in a sympathetic hug. I assumed the gesture was about my dad, which I had hoped was already so last year, when she said, "Oh, Alex, I'm so sorry about Becca."

"It was just a fight. I'm over it. What's to be sorry about?"

"You don't know?" She backed off the hug and looked at me with concern.

"Know what? What happened to Becca?" My heart leaped. Was she dead, too?

"I thought you'd know, since you guys are best friends—"

"Yes, yes, and she fucked my boyfriend. The end. What the hell is wrong with her?"

The problem with being friends with so many people from the drama department was that there was always drama. I had no patience for games of communication. Jenna looked around, frazzled, so I grabbed her shoulders and shook. "What. The. Fuck. Happened. To. Becca?"

She looked genuinely terrified, like I was going to bite off her ear. Which I actually felt like doing. She managed to eke out the worst string of words I'd heard since my dad died. And all of them before that day, too.

"Becca has cancer."

CHAPTER

I'D GONE DEAF. I couldn't hear anything around me after Jenna uttered those three little words. That's not true. I *could* hear those three little words over and over in my head. *Becca has cancer Becca has cancer Becca has cancer Becca has cancer.* Did deaf people hear words in their heads, too? All around me I watched in frenetic motion as people hugged their tanned, post-summer hellos, and all I wanted to do was fold my body up and stuff myself into my narrow locker.

"You didn't know?" I made out Jenna's muffled reply, and I responded with a wobbly head shake. She enveloped me in her newly thin arms, my own arms pinned to my side. I didn't have the ability to move them even if I wanted to hug her back. Which I didn't.

The bell rang, and students scattered. The first day of school was the only day everyone seemed to want to be on time to first period.

"I gotta go. You gonna be okay?" I'm sure Jenna's concern was sincere, but it felt hollow. A nod from me to her, and Jenna was off down the hall. I managed to stuff my empty backpack into my locker and remembered to grab a pen and notebook before I zombie-walked to advisory.

While everyone around me chattered about vacations, parties, hookups, and breakups, I doodled on the cover of my pristine red notebook. *Cancer*, I scratched. What did I know about cancer? I knew one of my mom's best friends died from it. I also knew a couple of my mom's friends who lived through it. So that was encouraging: Not everyone with cancer dies.

Then why did it equal death in my head? Why did it hit me in my stomach and make me cave in on myself when I heard Becca had it?

I didn't even know what kind of cancer she had. Were some kinds better than others? Would she lose a boob? Her hair?

Becca loved her hair.

I was never one to fawn over my straight, dark brown hair, and the second my mom allowed me to choose my own hairstyle I lobbed it off into a bob. I'd been through short and spiky, asymmetrical and edgy, shaggy, up through my latest look: blunt bangs and a nub of a ponytail, inspired by my favorite character, Kelly, from the brilliant British zombie miniseries, *Dead Set*.

But Becca was attached to her hair beyond its roots. She only allowed her mom to trim it after the fourth-grade gender-bending play. What wasn't to love about Becca's hair? It was dirty blond, almost waist-length, wavy most days, curly when she curled it, straight when she straightened it. She felt it gave her another prop with which to act. If she parted it on one side, it meant she was flirty. Down the middle: serious. High ponytail: fun. Low ponytail: somber. All of this I knew because I helped take her head shots for her résumé. Not that she had done any acting beyond school productions, but she wanted to be prepared.

What if she already lost her hair? What if I was so busy mourning the loss of my dad and the absence of an assnut boyfriend that I wasn't there for her when she needed me? What if all those times she tried to get in touch with me, she was asking for help? What if I was too late?

The bell signaling first period rang, and I let the push of the hallway crowds propel me to my next class. The bubbliness of my Spanish teacher, Señorita Goodwin, and the fiesta-themed decor of the room brought me out of my question-stalled brain for a short while.

I opened my notebook while people passed around this year's textbook and wrote:

THINGS I KNOW:
1) People don't always die from cancer
2) Becca is not dead, which I know because
   a) Her mom would have called me
   b) Jenna would not have spoken about
      her in the present tense

I was interrupted by the delivery of my new textbook, which I wrote my name in:

✝ Alex Buckley ✝

I always added the upside-down crosses, not because I was a Satanist but because I liked to imagine the next person to get my textbook wondering if somehow the book itself was evil. My legacy, if you will.

Thinking about my legacy made me think about death, which made me think about Becca.

I added one more item to my list:

3) Becca cannot die because my dad just died, and that would be much too shitty.

But was it enough to make it true?

CHAPTER

I **MANAGED TO SIT** through my first three classes before completely losing my shit. Instead of wading through the inanity of gym class the first week of school (it's always painful to watch the gym teacher try to locate her students among the five other classes sharing the gym, only to assign tiny lockers and reinforce uniform and deodorant rules), I walked to Becca's locker. Her full-sized one, not the gym-class one, where she forgot about a pair of socks last year and discovered that the locker room smell had, indeed, been her fault.

The administration at our high school was too lazy to reassign lockers each year, thus we retained the same locker, combination and all, the entire four years of high school. Perhaps that's why our school was rife with locker crime, although I blamed the idiots for leaving iPads and Kindles in their lockers. Becca and I had lockers nowhere near each other for alphabetical reasons. My locker section was filled with benign classmates ("benign" meant so much more than it used to) with whom I had shared three years of birthdays, breakups, breakdowns, and break-ins. Jenna Brown, of cancer announcement and weight loss fame, was particularly entertaining. If only I had thought to take a picture of her every day since freshman year. It would have made for a viral sensation, watching her shrink down.

Becca's locker section was a tangled pit of pompoms and sports gear, and I nearly missed thrusting my foot through the strings of Sean Shelby's tennis racket. He sneered at me, and I sneered right back. Nothing like an unpredictable, five-foot-two-inch chick to scare the sneer off a jackass jock's face. Maybe Sean remembered the time at Beth Sidell's Bat Mitzvah when I smacked him across the face after he tried to kiss me during the snowball dance.

He wasn't my type.

The electronic beep of the school bell cleared Becca's locker section relatively quickly, and I sunk down on the floor next to locker 353. I reached up and spun Becca's locker combination, then yanked open the locker to find it empty. Even though we kept the same lockers, the powers that be insisted we cleaned them out before we left for the summer. In case we moved.

Or died.

I hooked my finger through the lock hole and dangled my arm above my head, leaning against it as support.

Maybe it was nothing. Maybe she didn't even have cancer. Maybe it was just some ploy to get me to call her. She did love drama in all forms.

I yanked myself up by my finger and slunk through the quiet hallways to my own locker. The hall monitors were usually busy at major intersections on the first day of school, ushering frazzled freshmen to and from their big kid classes. The combination on my locker wasn't even a series of numbers in my head at this point, just a memorized, measured distance between spins. I could do it with my eyes closed and had. Inside my sagging, empty, first day of school backpack was my phone, off-limits during school hours or guaranteed confiscation, a rule solidified by last year's infamous Trig Texting Scandal. Even if I got caught, what could I possibly be texting the answers to on the first day of school? My gym locker combination? Someone's What I Did Over the Summer essay?

As I dialed Becca's cell, my entire body tensed at the prospect of speaking to her after two months of silence. And not just speaking to her, but speaking to her about having *cancer*.

To my sort-of relief, she didn't answer. I hung up, having too much to say in a message. I thought about calling her home line, but the possibility of talking to her mom about her daughter having cancer felt too meltdown-inducing for a hallway on the first day of school.

Footsteps from somewhere down the hall forced me to toss my phone back into my locker. I was jumpy as hell, with no answers and no inspiration for an excuse as to why I wasn't in class. When the feet that were stepping finally made their physical appearance, I saw the worn, black Chucks of Leo Dietz, a senior with rusty red hair who wore the same tattered tan army jacket come sun or snow. Leo intrigued me ever since I saw him leaving a midnight showing of *Evil Dead 2*. Horror movies were my one thing, my grotesque passion and pastime, especially classically gory yet hilarious ones like *Evil Dead 2*. I spent the entire summer poring through online collections of brilliantly titled movies like *Rabid Grannies* and *Frankenhooker*. They were the things that helped keep me sane when everything was so *in*sane. Leo and I made eye contact that night, but I was with Doug Dunhill, another ex, tongue permanently affixed to my ear. It pissed me off that Leo thought that was the company I kept. If he thought about me at all. I dumped Doug later that evening (morning, really) after he touched my boob one too many times without my blessing.

When Leo passed me at my locker, I caught a hint of his green eyes. I couldn't tell if they were looking at me. Then he walked completely out of sight, and I sagged a little at my inappropriate hope. What had I hoped for anyway? Thinking about Leo and horror movies was wrong at a time when I was supposed to be consoling or assisting or mourning my best friend who may or may not have cancer.

The footsteps that should have been getting fainter became louder again. And then Leo reappeared, looking at me with that intense, serious look he always had. As many scary movies as I watched, Leo's gaze made my heart beat harder than any of them. He must have been at least six foot three, maybe four. At five two, I was petite but not dainty, at least I liked to think. Still, it helped his imposing presence. He stuck his left hand into his jacket pocket and with two fingers pulled out a cigarette. "Smoke?" he asked, and I almost looked around me to see who he was talking to. Since it had never been me.

My brain Jell-O, all I managed to say was, "No. I don't smoke."

He shrugged, tucked the cigarette behind his ear, and walked away. For good that time.

If things were different, would I have thought more clearly to accept his offer? Not that I smoked. Or liked when other people smoked. Or normally ditched class.

I wasn't going to allow myself to think any further about Leo. Not until I could get to Becca. Wherever or however she was.

CHAPTER

AFTER SCHOOL I CAUGHT JENNA in the hall. She wasn't easy to find, with her dwindling size and her always-abuzz social persona. I discovered her in a locker section one over from mine, regaling with woe what I assumed was Becca's story—my story to hear, and certainly not hers to tell. When she saw me, she actually let out a "Ssshhh!" to the gathered crowd, and the people sea parted to allow me by. "Jenna." I glanced around at the group she had amassed, mostly drama club folk who I only knew from visits to Becca backstage. Freshman year I joined stage crew, but when I learned about the long hours required I quit. I already had my time-sucker of horror movies, whether it was watching or attempting to write my own. Spending my weeknights in the catwalk with a bunch of people dressed in all black versus splayed across my bed watching *Basket Case* was a no-brainer.

I never knocked Becca for her acting aspirations, nor did she knock me for my filmmaking dreams. It actually worked out perfectly, seeing as I always had an actress for my movies and she then had experience for her college applications. Or her résumé. Sometimes Becca spoke grandiosely about her dream to skip college altogether and make it straight to Hollywood, do not pass go, do not even wait tables until her big break. Becca strictly believed in becoming famous instantly, and I never for a moment doubted she could manage it.

If she made it that long.

"Can we talk away from your mob scene, please?" I looked directly at Jenna, not wanting to inadvertently make eye contact with any of her gang. Looks of pity weren't helpful. I needed facts, of which I had approximately none. She excused her entourage with a flick of her wrist. It made me smile. Two years and six jean sizes ago, Jenna was the chubby girl who only landed the supporting cast roles of mother, grandmother, or, once, uncle. Here she was, thirty pounds lighter, leading a group of underclassmen around like baby pull toys.

When we were relatively alone, aside from the people whose actual lockers were housed in that section, Jenna placed her hand on my shoulder and assured me, "Anything you need, Alex, I'm here for you."

Gag. "What I don't need is this bullshit pity party you're throwing me. I need details, Jenna. What do you actually know?"

She straightened herself up, a little insulted, but still the Keeper of Information. Then she transitioned into gossip mode, complete with hand held next to her mouth as if she were hiding the news from those only on one side of her. Drama divas. "My mom takes pilates with Becca's mom, and she told her that at the beginning of the summer Becca started to get sick. Like, sick all the time. They thought it was all sorts of things, like a pulled muscle and the flu and asthma, and finally she was in so much pain and they ended up in the hospital, draining fluid from her chest."

"Jesus fuck." My stomach turned. "Is she going through chemo? Is that what she has to do?" My knowledge of cancer was limited to what I read in books, watched on TV, and remembered from my mom's friends. But, really, it wasn't much. All I knew was wigs and death and probably a whole lot of awful in between.

"She started her first round this week. That's why she's not at school. Do you want me to give a message to my mom to give to her mom?"

That pissed me off. Just because I didn't know anything didn't mean that Jenna's mom had some sort of one-up on me when it came to Becca. "No. I'm going over there now."

"You sure? I don't know if Becca wants visitors."

"That'll do, Donkey," I warned Jenna. She meekly accepted defeat. I knew she meant well, but this was my best friend she was talking about. Estranged, maybe, but that would be over once I saw her.

Would she be bald? Hooked up to a machine? Gorier than the goriest of my horror movies? I felt utterly clueless.

I found my dad's station wagon in the parking lot, bequeathed to me by my mom after his death. She said that my having a car would help alleviate some of the stress of trying to get everyone everywhere. It may have alleviated that stress, but the idea of me driving after my dad was killed in a car accident had my mom shaken *and* stirred. I tried to quell some of the anxiety by reminding her that he wasn't wearing a seat belt, and he was in a taxi, being driven by someone we didn't know. Mom trained me as a road warrior herself, and I wouldn't dare leave the garage, or anywhere else, without a seat belt. That I promised her. She made me ditch my nicely aged Ford Escort for the upgrade to the safety-sealed Volvo. It was fine for driving to school, work, and the library, pretty much all I did. My brothers took most of Mom's energy, which wasn't entirely bad. At least she was forced to focus on something other than my dead dad. Too bad they were mutant turds with skateboards.

I drove on autopilot to Becca's. The traffic gods were kind, and I made it to her house quickly. I parked my car on the street outside Becca's house, just in case someone needed to get in or out of the garage in a hurry. Becca lived on a quiet cul-de-sac in one of the nicer subdivisions that fed into our high school. I lived in a one-step-down subdivision, which meant that the houses were a little older and a little smaller. Becca had the good fortune of having her own bathroom, being the only child. Did good fortune matter if you were the one with cancer?

Instead of sitting dazed in my car, I decided on the rip-the-Band-Aid-off approach and forced myself to get out. The doorbell, a classic ding-dong edition versus the bleepy, robotic one my dad installed at our house, rang in the pit of my stomach. The anticipation of *are they home or not* hung in the air, until the telltale shuffle of Becca's mom's slippers (it was a take-your-shoes-off-when-you-enter house) approached the door. Upon seeing me, her tired face brightened, and she opened the screen door and ushered me in. Before I could say "sorry," or, "Is Becca home?" or whatever the appropriate thing was that wasn't coming out of my mouth, Mrs. Mason enveloped me in her lean arms and said, "Alex, so good to see you. Becca missed you. I knew you'd fix whatever it was that you were fighting about this time."

Not surprising that Becca didn't tell her mom this particular fight had her sleeping with my boyfriend, so I said, "Yeah. I just needed some time."

"Of course. Becca is upstairs. She might be sleeping, but I'm sure she'll want to see you. Go right up."

Maybe I had wanted Mrs. Mason to detain me for longer, tell me all that I'd missed or ask me how my family was doing or even reprimand me for staying away so long. I didn't expect heading up to my best friend's room so soon to be so difficult. My best friend, Becca, who had cancer.

CHAPTER

I IMAGINED BECCA in the center of a giant, four-poster canopy bed, so tiny and sickly that the bed practically engulfed her. None of that made sense, since Becca neither had a four-poster bed nor a canopy. In fact, she constantly bitched about the fact that her bed was merely a twin on a metal bed frame. It was a hilarious argument I witnessed between her and her mother.

"Mom, I'm getting close to adulthood now. Don't you think that warrants a queen? Or at least a double?"

"My dear," her mom pronounced, "you are no queen, and giving you a bigger bed just gives you license to share it with someone else."

Touché.

"Knock knock," I said and did. My heart beat behind my eyes, and my stomach hovered around the middle of my chest. I hoped whatever I saw behind that door wasn't like something out of *The Exorcist*. Pea soup grossed me out.

"Come in," said a familiar voice. Becca's voice. Who else would it be?

I opened the door with a jerk, not purposely, but my hands also seemed not quite in working order. The back of the door slammed into the wall as it flew open. A picture hanging behind the door jumped off the wall and landed with a smash.

"Shit. Sorry," I said, trying to pick up the pieces.

"Does that mean you're still mad at me?" Becca asked from the corner of her room, where she sat in her big blue comfy chair, hidden under a blanket her grandma had knitted. The only parts of her exposed were her arms, which held a PS3 controller, and her head, which looked surprisingly the same as the last time I saw her.

"Are you kidding?" I asked, gingerly closing the door behind me and stepping over the broken frame containing a picture of the two of us from eighth-grade graduation. "How can I still be mad at you?"

"So cancer absolved me of everything? Shit, I should have gotten cancer a long time ago."

"Ha ha." I wasn't ready to joke about Becca having cancer, and I was a bit put off that she was. I sat on the edge of her bed and dangled my feet. "I was all ready to forgive you when I came to school today, but apparently you had to go all drama department on me." That was me attempting to be light, but it was a stretch. "What's going on, Becca?"

"What don't you know?" She assessed how far the rumor mill had gotten.

"All I know is what Jenna told me, which wasn't enough. She said you had cancer and that you started chemo today. I don't even really know what that means. And you look okay." I looked at Becca's face and recognized a tiredness and an unfamiliar fear in her eyes that I hadn't noticed a second ago. I averted my glance to the television screen where she had her game paused. Two medieval-looking people were frozen, strategically placed pixels obscuring the sexual deviancy on her tv. "Lovely, Becca. Are you just faking cancer so you can watch digitized people get it on?"

"If only," she sighed, threw down her controller, and began to cough an extended, pained cough. When it subsided, she said, "It is pretty sick that I can do this while you're in school, though, isn't it? My mom walked in on me today mid-sex scene, and she said, 'You have as much computer-animated sex as you like, honey.'"

I laughed, but switched gears quickly. "So was Jenna right about the chemo?"

"No, of course she wasn't. I mean, yes, I'm having chemo, but not until tomorrow. So you can tell her know-it-all ass that she got something wrong. Fuck. She's probably planning her audition scene for the fall play."

"Who cares about that, Becca?" It felt like the two of us were avoiding the actual cancer discussion no matter how many times we brought it up or got close. But my stomach, heart, and hands wouldn't get back to normal without knowing what the hell was going on. "Tell me what happened."

"The long or short version?"

"Long, if you want to tell it."

"It involves someone and some events that I probably shouldn't bring up."

"Davis, I'm assuming? He's bagged and tagged to me. Speak about him freely."

"If you're sure," she checked. I nodded the okay. "After we, you know, after your dad's, you know, he kept calling me. And at first, I told him to leave me alone. But when you wouldn't talk to me, I don't know, I guess I was pissed at you, so Davis and I sort of hung out a bunch over the summer. Not really hung out in an intellectually stimulating way. More of an . . ." Becca pointed to the computerized sex on her TV. "That kind of way."

I shuddered and grimaced, but I couldn't fault her. Davis repulsed me at that point, and, well, Becca had cancer.

"I know this must suck to hear, and believe me it gets grosser."

"I can't imagine how, but go ahead. 'It gets grosser' is such an intriguing setup."

"He was visiting down south"—she gestured to the crotchy portion of her body—"and he found some lumps. All very sexy, of course. I checked them out in the mirror later on, mortified I had some disgusting zit infestation or something. But they weren't zitty, really, and then I realized I had them in other places, too. So my mom made an appointment for me at the doctor."

"You told your mom Davis found lumps while deep-sea diving?"

"God no! I didn't tell her how I found them, and she didn't ask. After that it was like a shitstorm of doctor appointments and tests. The biopsy was fucking horrific. They seemed to want to rule everything else out before they went with the capital-C cancer diagnosis. Do you want more gory details about my summer?"

Gore, as in horror-movie-blood-and-guts-made-of-corn-syrup, I could handle. But after Dad's death and the real-life gore of that, I could do without. "Why don't you skip to what they said," I told her.

"They said I have Hodgkin's lymphoma, which they claimed is very treatable. So, yay me, I guess." She didn't look "yay me." She looked petrified.

"That sounds promising," I hoped.

"I guess, except that I still have to go through chemo, which, if everything I read about it online is true—"

"Which it never is," I unhelpfully interjected.

"—is going to suck oversized donkey balls," Becca continued.

"You *have* been hanging around Davis." I rolled my eyes.

"Sorry," she said.

"No. It's okay. If Davis's donkey balls help you get through cancer, then suck them all you like." Becca threw a pillow at me.

"You know he stopped calling after I figured out it was cancer. Something like his next-door neighbor died of cancer, and he couldn't handle it."

"Sorry," I told her. "He bailed on me, too, obviously."

"He's gone now. Joined the army."

"What? When? We both dated a guy that's in the army? That's so weird. I'm a pacifist, for fuck's sake."

Our eyes floated over to the two sexing computer creations on her TV. "Dude, you need to turn that off. It's so wrong."

"Says you," she uttered, but turned off the screen.

"So you go for chemo tomorrow? What exactly is chemo?"

"They explained it to me, but I only hear every sixteenth word when the doctors are talking. It's so surreal. Like a TV show moment. *You have cancer.* And then I'm supposed to listen to someone explain a million billion things to me? What I got was that they inject me with a bunch of different drugs for a week that attack the cancer. Then I get at least a two-week break so my body doesn't completely shut down, which sounds delightful because I'll probably be puking and gross the entire time. And then I go back and go through it all again. And again. They said I need at least four rounds. I'm pretty freaked out."

"Is there anything I can do?" I asked. A stupid question that too many people asked me after my dad died. I would have taken the chemo for her if I could.

"No, I don't think so. But if I don't call or text you this week, don't be upset, okay? I have no idea what I'll be like."

"I could bring you stuff. Crappy magazines and chicken soup?" It was all I could pitifully think to offer.

"Maybe. I'll let you know. I've heard it can really get ugly."

"You'll never be ugly, Becca," I assured her.

"I said *it* can get ugly, not *I* could." She laughed a little, then choked on the laugh and coughed some more. Her eyes welled with tears. "I'm going to lose my hair, Alex."

I deflated for Becca. *That hair.* If I had cancer, I could do without my hair. I had gone pretty close to no hair a couple of times. But Becca's hair was too bountiful. "Alex?" She looked at me for help. "I want you to shave my head."

CHAPTER

"YOU WANT TO SHAVE your head? Why? Is your hair definitely going to fall out?" Cancer had so many preconceptions, so many things that I've heard about through passing Yahoo! articles I never bothered to read, movies I didn't want to watch. Why depress myself? And here I was, living it. Or, not living it. Instead, watching it possibly devour my best friend.

"My hair will fall out. Fact. I don't want to wake up with chunks of hair stuck to my pillow. This way, I control things."

I understood that. Control in any situation is important; in one where you pretty much have none: imperative. "But maybe it won't fall out," I tried to reason, with no logic behind it.

"It will, and it will suck." She stood up slowly off her chair. She moved more cautiously than I was used to. "Whatever they inject in me during chemo is attacking my cells, including the cells that do this." She flipped the bottom of her bouncy, thick, nearly waist-length hair. A vacant and glassy expression let me know that as cool as she was being, she was not entirely one with the cucumber.

"Do you have a razor? Not, like, the leg kind, but for your head?"

"My mom bought one for me yesterday. She was totally crying because my soul lives in my hair, apparently. I'll go get it." Was that supposed to be funny? Was there a manual for this somewhere, *How to Respond to People with Cancer*, because I didn't know what was appropriate and what was just plain off. Like when my dad died, and every person said they were sorry. I get that that's the polite thing to say, but after a while it sounded so insincere. Just once I wanted someone to be honest, tell me that they couldn't imagine what it felt like to one second have a dad, and the next second have a pile of body parts and insurance money that'll pay for the college of my dreams. Would Dad even know if I went to college now?

I almost said something to Becca then about my dad, how I missed him or felt confused or even hated him sometimes for leaving just when I really needed him to lean on, but how did that make sense when the reasons I needed him all had to do with the cancer sufferer standing in front of me with a brand-new electric razor in her hands?

"Where should we do this?" she asked. I noticed a twitch in her hand, and I didn't know if it was nerves or something to do with the cancer. I guessed nerves were technically something to do with the cancer. "Seeing as you're the expert and all."

That made me feel guilty. The fact that I'd shaved my head before, just to change things up, made me feel like a dick, as if it was insensitive of me. Did Becca see it that way? That only people who have to shave their head should be allowed to do so, otherwise it was just belittling the magnitude of losing one's hair?

Or was I overthinking?

I chose to believe the latter and that, of the two of us, I technically was closer to being a professional head shaver than Becca was. "Do you have any garbage bags? The big black kind?"

"In the kitchen." She sat down heavily on a rolling desk chair. "Would you mind getting them?"

"No, of course not. Need anything else?" She shook her head. "Why don't you check in on your humping game pals, and I'll be right back." That got a smile out of her.

Becca's mom stood in the kitchen cradling a steaming mug in her hands and staring out the window. In days BC (before cancer) I wouldn't have hesitated to barge into the room, ask where the garbage bags were, and go on my merry way. But what if she was crying? And all I could offer her was a "sorry"? Thankfully, Mrs. Mason turned around and saw me, a drooped but tearless look on her face. "Hi, Alex, does she need something?" Obviously, Becca was at the forefront of her brain.

"We're about to shave her head, and I came to get some black garbage bags for the mess. Under the sink, right?" I let myself into the cabinet and pulled out several bags. When I stood up, Becca's mom was close by with a gallon Ziploc bag in her hands.

"Save some of it, please. In here." If this were a horror movie, the moment could have been so creepy: the obsessive mom wanting to save lost locks of her daughter's hair. Instead, it forced a lump to my throat.

"Thanks." I grabbed the bag before the two of us lost our shit and ran back upstairs. Becca was in the same hunched position in her desk chair, no romping computer people to be seen.

"Got the bags. And your mom wants me to save your hair in this." I held up the Ziploc.

"Weird. She better not give it away. I know they make wigs out of hair for cancer patients, but, shit, it's my hair. And I'm already a cancer fucking patient." She seemed angry for the first time today. If it were me, anger would have been my first, second, and third response to every step of this. Becca was still so composed.

"It *is* your hair. You should make a coat out of it or something," I suggested as I cut a hole in one of the garbage bags. I pulled the bag down over her head to keep the hair off her pajamas. I ripped two other bags down their seams and spread them under the chair.

"Get that mirror, will you?" She pointed to a flimsy, full-length mirror that she used in various locales around her room to practice monologues. "I want to watch this." Her expression was resolute. When the mirror was in place in front of her, she said, "I don't think I have enough for a coat. Maybe a vest." It could have been funny, if she'd smiled the tiniest bit when she said it.

"I'm going to use scissors before I hit the clippers, if that's okay. Then they won't get clogged." I pulled a pair of red-handled scissors out of a drama camp mug on her desk.

"Give me a bob first, will you? I've always wanted to try one. Haven't had the guts to go that short since that awful haircut in elementary school."

"I'll do my best." I pulled all of Becca's hair behind her head into a low ponytail, then started cutting with the scissors. "Damn. Do you have any sharper scissors? These are weak."

"Just keep going, okay?" Becca's eyes were wide as some of the newly shorn strands escaped the hold of my hands and dangled around her face. Eventually, I hacked my way through the dense ponytail and held it up.

"We got one, Pa," I drawled as if I just cut the tail off a raccoon.

Becca said nothing, just turned her head side to side to look at her drastically shorter hair. "Kind of cute, right? I can rock this. When my hair grows back," she convinced herself, as I bagged the ponytail in her mom's commemorative Ziploc.

"Now for the buzzing," I announced. "These razors have different length attachments. Which do you want?"

"The shortest one but not totally bald. I'd like to be fuzzy for as long as possible," Becca told me.

I plugged in the razor and flicked on the switch. The razor jumped to life in my hand. I approached Becca's head. "Ready?" I asked.

She inhaled deeply, in her actorly way, and then stuck out her hand. "I'll do it."

I didn't ask if she needed help, just handed her the vibrating razor. Without hesitation, she attacked her hair on the right side of her head. Clumps fell off onto the garbage bags with a puff. When she approached the center, she changed sides and buzzed the left. Eventually, only a Mohawk remained.

"I almost look tough, don't I?" She looked at me in the mirror.

"Badass," I agreed.

Then down came the Mohawk.

In the end, a short fuzz remained of Becca's once lustrous, long hair.

"I don't know why," I said, "but I just envisioned myself swallowing all the hair on the ground and choking to death."

"Time to lay off the horror movies, Alex." I actually pulled a tiny smile from her. She looked really pretty, hair be damned.

"Want me to shave mine now? In solidarity?" I asked. "'Cause I don't mind."

She turned in her chair to look at me instead of my reflection. "It doesn't mean anything if you shave your head, Alex, because you would shave your head even if I didn't have cancer."

"True." I looked down at the hairy mess.

"Instead, you should wear a really long, glamorous wig." I widened my eyes in a horrified manner. "I'm just kidding. God. You'd think I asked you to have sex with my boyfriend and then get cancer or something."

We both laughed. Maybe it wasn't funny, but standing next to heaps of Becca's hair while barely any was on her head, it felt a lot better than crying.

"I have one more thing I need you to do." Becca was serious as I gathered the garbage bags from the floor.

"Sure. What? Anything."

"Put down my hair, and sit. This is important."

I dropped the garbage bags, and fluffs of hair exploded from the mess.

"What? You're not going to put me in your will, are you? Because you're not going to die," I told her.

"Maybe. Maybe not. But I don't have a will. I wrote something else. And I need you to help me with it."

"What? Do you want me to kill someone?" I asked nervously.

"Alex, shut up. Although, I'll keep that in mind. No, I wrote a bucket list. And I need you to help me do it."

CHAPTER

"**A BUCKET LIST?** Like something an old man writes when he retires? Bungee jumping and shit?"

"Not only old men write bucket lists, Alex. And I already went bungee jumping when my family went to Acapulco."

"So what are you talking about?"

"Stuff I want to do before I die. Not only old people die, you know."

"I'm thoroughly aware of that, thank you." I pursed my lips at the thought that my dad, while parently old, would never have been considered an old man.

"All the more reason to do a bucket list. We have no idea how much time any of us have left, and what if we don't get to do all of the things we dreamed we'd do?"

"Big fucking deal. Then we'll be dead in a box, in the ground, not knowing any better. Actually, I'm thinking cremation and having my ashes sprinkled on the Peter Pan ride at Disneyland. But don't tell anyone."

"I'll take it to the grave." Becca smirked.

"Why are we even talking about this? You are not going to die. You are not. Going. To. Die." I stood up and started to pace, kicking at broken pieces of frame glass along the way.

"Let's say I'm not, for the sheer joy of being not dead, but that doesn't mean we shouldn't be doing amazing things."

"Amazing things? You want me to build a well in a Third World country?" I stopped pacing long enough to give her my patented *you've got to be kidding* look.

"Your kindness shines through your blackened exterior, Alex." I flipped Becca off. "Maybe not amazing, but we have to do what we want and not let conventional fear get in the way. Like when we were freshmen, remember when Channing Tatum was at an appearance at a bookstore because he wrote a page or something in a book on dancing, and you totally wanted to go . . ."

"I thought we promised not to talk about that."

"I'm playing the cancer card and bringing it back."

"How gloriously thoughtful of you," I drolled.

"I know, right? Anyway, you had that box with all of those pictures of him in the secret hole in your closet, but you refused to go see him. And you cried, remember? Because you regretted not going."

"I did not cry." I sat down again at the degrading memory.

"Two tears, but for you that's extreme." I shrugged because I knew she was right. "We should never have any regrets, not when we're dying and not when we're alive. Like Ke$ha so wisely puts it, 'Let's make the most of the night like we're gonna die young.'" Becca looked so determined, I couldn't fault her for quoting Ke$ha.

"Does this mean you want me to write a bucket list, and we'll drop out of school together and travel the world pursuing our sick and twisted fantasies and then drive off a cliff holding hands?"

"Take it down a notch, Alex. Your bucket list can wait. I'm the one dying here."

"I'll only help you if you stop fucking saying that."

"I like saying it. The more I say it, the less real it sounds."

"Fair enough. What do I have to do?"

Becca waved me over to her bed with a floppy hand, and I scrunched in next to her. Even without hair, I could smell her shampoo, citrusy and fresh, almost good enough to eat.

She reached underneath her mattress and pulled out a crinkled piece of Hello Kitty stationery I vaguely remembered giving her for her birthday in elementary school.

"This is my bucket list. I've been writing it since I was nine," Becca shared.

"And *I'm* the morbid one?" I raised my eyebrows.

"Yes. I'm not the one who used a needle and pen to tattoo their thigh with a smiley face."

"It's not a smiley face. It's a dead guy smiley face. That's what the X's instead of eyes mean."

"Yeah, like I said, morbid. The point was—"

"There was a point?" I laughed a little.

"Alex, we're running out of time. *I'm* running out of time. Tomorrow is it. Whatever happens, I have no idea what it's going to be like or how long or what I'll look like or when I'll see you again, so we need to do this now." Becca had worked herself up, or I had, and she started coughing. When she didn't stop after a few hacks, her mom's feet pounded up the stairs.

"Here, honey." Becca's mom reached for a small pitcher on her nightstand, and, with shaking hands, poured a glass of water. Becca drank it slowly, deliberately, until the glass was emptied and her mom filled it again.

"Thanks, Mom." Becca sounded younger and sweeter, like a little kid version of Becca I remembered from when she had a broken arm and she worked the pity factor to get a massive Polly Pocket yacht. But this didn't feel like working it. She was already becoming a smaller, frightened version of herself.

"Alex, Becca needs to get her rest for tomorrow. I hate to ask, but I think you should probably go."

Becca snapped out of her Polly Pocket pity voice for a moment. "Mom, I need to keep talking to Alex. I might not see her for a while." She looked at me. "The doctors said I'd be really out of it. And I can't risk bringing germs into the house because of my weakened immune system. You won't want to see me all gross and gnarly anyway," she assumed, turning to me.

"Gross and gnarly is my business, Becca. But whatever you need me to do."

"Fifteen minutes more, Mom?" Becca opened her eyes wide in their most manipulative, manga-like expression.

"Your hair—" It was as though Becca's mom just noticed the mass of missing locks. Tears and shudders erupted from her, the absolute worst thing to watch. I knew parents are supposed to be human and all, but I wish she could have pulled it together for Becca's sake. And mine.

"I saved some in a bag for you." I tried to cheer Becca's mom up and held the bag out for her to see. Apparently, that wasn't the correct thing to do. The sobs and shudders turned even more extreme.

"Mom, you're freaking Alex out, and I just got her back. Can you please give us fifteen minutes alone? I'm fine without the hair. Just pretend it's for a big role starring opposite Hugh Jackman." Becca always knew the right thing to say, and I saw the smile I had hoped for spread across her mom's face. She loved Hugh Jackman.

"Fifteen minutes," she agreed, and grabbed a handful of tissues on her way out.

"And you wonder why I'm in drama," Becca sighed after her mom closed the door.

"The list?" I had to know where she was going with this.

"Yeah, so I've been doing this since I was nine. Not, like, as an *I'm going to die* list but more like a list of things I need to do someday."

"Before you die," I pushed.

"Well, I sure as fuck can't do them after I die."

"Says you. What if I learn the art of taxidermy, stuff you, and take you with me everywhere I go until we complete the list?"

"You're totally going to turn that into a movie someday, aren't you?"

"Probably."

"You can use my dead body as the dead body," Becca volunteered.

"You'll be too busy starring as the gorgeous, *living* friend. Who is alive. And not dead at all."

"Okay, good, because that's on my list." She pointed to number 19: Star in one of Alex's movies, and have it seen by actual people instead of just me and Alex. "Sorry," she noticed. "My bucket list isn't very well-worded."

"Can we stop calling it a bucket list? Again: implied death," I noted.

"I thought it meant all the things you can fit into a bucket to do."

"Um, no, I think it means all the things you can do before you kick the bucket. Which, actually, I think is an allusion to suicide, right? Like, kicking the bucket out from under your feet while you hang. Or maybe someone else is kicking out the bucket?"

"Yuck and gross and eeww."

"So no more bucket. How about the Fuck-It List? Like, fuck it, I might die, so let me look like an idiot doing all sorts of ridiculous things?"

"The Fuck-It List. Noble, but with a hint of edge to it."

"Think they'd ever let me name a movie *The Fuck-It List*?"

"Probably not. They'd be all, 'How about *The Stuff-It List*? That's how kids these days really talk, right?'" Becca perfectly adopted a hilariously oblivious male executive's voice.

From downstairs we heard Becca's mom yell, "Ten minutes!"

"Damn, woman. She's probably got her stopwatch ticking. Okay, we need to focus. I don't know how much of the list I can do by myself in a short amount of time, so I had the idea that maybe you could help me out with some things on it and I could live vicariously through you."

I grabbed the list and skimmed through the scribbles written over every possible inch of the worn paper. "No way in hell am I sending my bra to Zac Efron." I gagged.

"Shut up. I was like twelve when I wrote that."

"Did you even have boobs?"

"I had a training bra. I think SpongeBob was on it. Anyway, you don't have to do everything, but, like, here, number thirteen." She pointed to a line written in pink pen. "Sleep on a beach to watch the sunset and sunrise. You could definitely manage that."

"So could you! Come on!" I prodded. It was hard for me to

imagine Becca being so sick, or maybe not even here to do something so simple.

"Alex, humor me. Things on this list need to start getting done, so I can feel like I accomplished something just in case I do die. And don't give me that shit that I'll be dead so I won't know whether or not I accomplished anything because now *you* will know and you'll have to live with it weighing on your lightly existing conscience."

"Geez, fine. No need to bring my conscience into this. I'll sleep on a beach. I'll be a regular beach bum. I'll bring you back a grain of sand and everything."

"This is serious, Alex. You can't just do it half-assed. Do everything like it's your last night on Earth."

"Are you going to quote Ke$ha again? Fine. Two grains of sand." Becca smacked my shoulder. "Isn't there anything on here we could take care of now? So you can do some of it?" I scanned the page. Numbers and sentences in various colored pens and markers were strewn every which way. "Here! I found one. Number eight: Crank call Adam Levitz."

"That's on the list? God, I was such a douchey nine-year-old."

Adam Levitz was a crush gone wrong in fourth grade. He invited Becca to the Fun Fair at our elementary school, but when he didn't pick her up at her house she and I went to the school in hopes of meeting him there. Turned out it was all a trick masterminded by Queen Bitch Mara Radnor. Apparently, Becca hadn't gotten over it.

"It's on the list. Let's do it." I reached for Becca's phone and punched in *67, so her number would show up as private.

"Give me that." Becca grabbed the phone out of my hands and dialed some numbers.

"Why do you still know his phone number?" I was incredulous.

"I tried calling him so many times that night he ditched me, it stayed in my head. Ssshhh—" Becca held up a finger to quiet me. In a hilariously sexy, breathy voice, Becca asked, "Is Adam there? No? Well, can you tell him Cassandra called, and I just wanted to let him know he gave me chlamydia. Thanks."

We both started giggling when she hung up. "That was weird," I told her.

"I know. Cassandra's such a tramp."

"Cross it off." I pushed the list at her along with a pen from her nightstand. "Let's do one more," I suggested. "We have five minutes. Is there a quick one? Like where we make out or something?" I asked.

"What? That's not on there, is it?" Becca scanned the list. "How about this one?" Number fifteen: Flash the homeschool boy next door."

Becca lived next to a family with six girls and one boy, all home-schooled. We knew nothing about them except that the boy was our age, ridiculously hot, and his bedroom window lined up perfectly with Becca's.

"You little whore. You have to do this one." I nudged her.

"I don't know. Is it too skanky?"

"It's not like your list said to give the homeschool boy a handjob. Unless that's further down. Ha. Get it? Further down?"

"Alex! Time to go!" Becca's mom called once again from downstairs.

"Your mom is insane, by the way," I told her.

Becca wasted no time answering me. Before I finished my sentence, she was on her feet and heading to her window.

"Oh my god. He's there. At his little homeschool desk facing his little homeschool window. He looked up. He sees me."

"No time like the present for a nip slip," I advised.

"I'm going to do it. I'm going to do it," Becca chanted. She threw her t-shirt to the floor. "I'm totally doing it. He's looking! I'm going to take off my bra. I'm going to do it. I'm going to do it."

"This play-by-play is really sexy, Becca," I teased.

Becca reached around her back and unhooked her bra. "Here I go. I'm taking off my bra. One. Two. Three." Becca flung her bra across her room and threw her arms up in the air. "He's smiling!"

"Yeah. I'd imagine so."

"I'm going to blow him a kiss." Becca did just that. Then her bedroom door opened, and her mom barged in. Becca spun around instantly, arms crossed over her chest. "Mom! Get out!" Becca screamed. "Alex is leaving! Give us a minute, damnit!"

I don't know if Becca's mom left because of what Becca said or because she didn't want to know what Becca was actually doing. We busted out laughing the second the door closed. Becca threw her shirt back on and climbed into bed.

"That was so excellent. See how good it's going to feel when you do these things for me?" She was really serious about me doing her list.

"I'm not showing my tits to your neighbor, Becca."

"You don't have to. I already did!" she squealed. "Calm thyself, Becca," she breathed, something she often did before a show to center herself. "You don't have to do all of them. I know it's a lot. Just some of them so you can report back to me. Really live while I can't."

"When you put it that way, I'm pretty much obligated to say yes, aren't I?"

"That's the idea."

"I better go, or your mom might try to smoke me out. Should we hug?" Hugging now felt too infinite.

"Yes, we should, and we will." Becca worked herself out of the bed and wrapped her arms around me. That did it. My hard candy shell melted into a puddle of chocolate in her arms. "I always knew you were a softy."

"Careful what you say. I've got a shiv in my pocket." I sniffed.

"I love you, Alex. You and your shiv."

"Love you, too, Becca. Even if I have to sleep on a beach to prove it."

"I hope you get sand in your undies," Becca whispered in my ear.

CHAPTER

WHEN I PARKED my dad's car in our empty garage, I knew I'd be home alone. But I didn't want to be. A note on the kitchen table read, "The boys have soccer. Be home by 8. Pizza in the freezer. Hope you had a good first day. Love you, Mom." The thought crossed my mind to actually watch my brothers' soccer game, but that momentary lapse of sport dementia quickly passed. I could've studied Becca's list, started my game plan, created a schedule. But maybe I didn't want to think about it, about anything. Instead, I opted for a pint of Cherry Garcia and a viewing of my comfort film *Dead Alive*. Most people know Peter Jackson as the director of the Lord of the Rings trilogy and *The Hobbit*, and rightly so because they're brilliant. I would argue even more brilliant is his early, and finest, film about a man in New Zealand whose mom gets bitten by a plague-infected monkey at the zoo. As a result, she turns into a festering, hungry horndog along with other not-so-upstanding members of town, and her son does his best to take care of them. Possibly one of the goriest films ever made, there is even a sweet love story, a hilarious running zombie baby, and a priest who yells, "I kick ass for the Lord!" Could there be anything better?

As much ice cream as I consumed from the too-tiny pint, and as mind-bogglingly sublime as *Dead Alive* was, I couldn't kick Becca out of my head. What was she doing at that moment? Was there any way to stop her from remembering that she had cancer? Was it completely unfair that I was using food and film to try to forget? How could I let myself forget when she had no choice?

I stirred the last of the ice cream into a nice soup, then tipped the cup back and chugged it. I had to get out of my quiet house. With the Fuck-It List folded in my back pocket, I got into my car.

I found something heavy on my MP3 player, someone screaming punishingly into my ears. I felt I deserved it, that here I was in my dad's car, alive when he was dead, healthy when my best friend had cancer. Who was I to be alive? Who decided? I cranked the music even louder to drown my thoughts. Admittedly, my head hurt, but I enjoyed the annoyed looks from the people pulled up next to me at stoplights. What did they know? Their lives were probably so simple. I glared at the back of a bald man's head in the car in front of me. *You deserve to be bald, bastard. Becca does not.*

My car led me to the parking lot of my old elementary school, Irving. The same school Becca and I attended together, where our friendship grew. Maybe if I sat there long enough, time would move backward and none of this cancer stuff would exist. Maybe even my dad would still be here. I closed my eyes and let the music consume me. My lips pursed tightly, willing my eyes not to cry.

BAM!

A loud pound on the glass shocked my eyes open, and I squinted at a figure hovering around my car window. The glare of the sun made him difficult to see, but I knew that military jacket from one too many hallway stares at Leo Dietz. He tried speaking to me, his straight lips moving but the sound drowned out by my music. I switched off the ignition, and he tried again.

"Rough day?" he asked, as he leaned slightly into my window.

"Why would you ask that? Do I look like shit or something?" I don't know why I said that, except that I was worried I did look like shit. Then I felt guilty for worrying about how I looked when Becca was awaiting her fate. I wondered if I'd ever have a guiltless thought again.

"Nah. You don't look like shit. I only listen to Lamb of God when I hate someone. Or myself." That's when I noticed a basketball tucked under his arm.

"You play basketball?" I asked with a hint of disgust in my voice. There was nothing less appealing to me than an ass-smacking member of a high school sports team.

"If you mean I know how to manipulate a basketball, then yes. But I'm not on a team or anything." His jacket smelled of stale cigarettes.

"Well, that's good. 'Cause I was about to ask you to leave if you said yes."

He smiled at me, a smile I'd never been that close to. His teeth weren't perfect. They weren't snaggletooth or stained, but his canine teeth stuck out a little farther than his front two. I chuckled to myself at the notion of him being a vampire, something Becca and I would have had a field day with.

"You want to shoot with me?" For a quick second I thought he meant guns, but he held the basketball up with the invite.

"Really?" I didn't know if my apprehension was because I hated sports or I didn't want to look stupid in front of him.

"Yeah. It's fun to play here because the baskets are so low. It makes me feel like a giant."

"You are a giant," I noted.

"Get out of the car already," he commanded. I obeyed.

This close, our height difference was noticeable. I had to look up to talk to him. I was glad it wasn't the other way around because that would make me on constant booger alert.

We walked together to the nearby basketball court, and he was right: It was kind of fun to feel superior to the baskets.

"This almost makes me want to join a basketball team," I told him as we lay down on a grassy berm for a rest. "Like, one for six-year-olds."

Leo laughed a small, inward laugh and pulled out a pack of cigarettes from his jacket pocket. He held the pack out to me as an offer. I hesitated. "When in Rome." I shrugged. "Or an elementary school parking lot."

He put both cigarettes in his mouth, lighting them at the same time. He passed one over to me, and I held it between my fingers. I never imagined a cigarette would feel so light and insignificant. It seemed like such a constant crutch in so many lives, I thought it would have more substance to it. I gingerly held the cigarette up to my lips, as it had been to Leo's, and took a tentative inhale. Then I coughed like the inexperienced asshole I was. "Damn. Why do you bother with this? My mouth tastes like I just sucked on a turd."

He laughed his quiet laugh again and said, "It gets better once you get used to it."

"That's stupid. That's like when someone tells you, 'He seems

like a prick at first, but he's really nice once you get to know him.'
Why bother?"

"I guess because it also gets addictive once you get used to it."

"What about"—I wished I didn't say it—"cancer?"

"It's just death, man. Cancer or not, I'll die." He lay back into the grass and puffed smoke into the sky.

I lay down next to him, my arm touching his jacket sleeve. I wondered if he could feel it. "I don't want to talk about death right now," I told him.

"What do you want to talk about?"

I kept the cigarette in my hand and tried flicking off the ashes as they burned in the wind. I didn't smoke any more of it.

"Did you go to school here?" I asked Leo.

"No. We moved away before and after grade school. My older brother, Jason, went here, though."

"He's in Afghanistan, right?" I asked, the not-so-subtle stalker.

"How'd you know?" he asked. When I paused to answer, he continued, "I don't want to talk about him right now."

"So what do *you* want to talk about?"

"You like horror movies, right?" Smoke wafted out of Leo's mouth as he spoke.

"Yeah. How'd you know?" *Welcome to the mutual stalkers society.* I tried not to sound giddy at the thought of Leo knowing something about me.

"I saw you last year at the midnight showing of *Evil Dead 2.*"

"You did?" I wanted to tell him that I saw him, too, but that felt too eager.

"Yep" was all he said.

"What's your favorite?" I asked.

"Horror movie?" he checked.

"Yeah. Your absolute favorite. Which one?"

"Is it too obvious to say *Evil Dead 2*?" He seemed less confident when I talked to him than when he stood around looking menacing and mysterious. I didn't know if I liked the vulnerability on him. Just like I hated it on me.

"Maybe a little predictable, but still a noble choice. Did you hear Bruce Campbell—"

"Is going to be at the Orpheum for *Army of Darkness*. I know. I'm stoked. Do you want to go?" I smirked at the possibility of a date until he added, "My friend Brian was supposed to go with me, but he's going out of town now. So I've got an extra ticket."

This wasn't quite how my fantasies went, but I'd take it. Horror movies were always more fun with someone else. And I didn't think Becca would make it. Would she be bummed that I was going out and she wasn't? Or would she want every detail of what it was like being near Leo? I wondered if there was a horror movie out there where someone gets killed by their own guilt.

"When is it?" I asked as if I didn't already know.

"Friday at seven. It's okay if you're busy. Just thought I'd ask." *Aren't we casual?*

"I planned on going, so sure. Yeah."

"Good," he replied.

We lay on our backs quietly for a couple of silent minutes, until Leo asked, "So what's yours?"

"Excuse me?" I asked.

"Your favorite."

"Oh yeah. I like *Dead Alive*. I think it's funnier than *Evil Dead* without trying as hard. Maybe it's the New Zealand accents."

"That's a good one. The lawn mower scene is killer."

"So good," I agreed.

Several more minutes of silence rolled by with the clouds. I didn't mind. Leo's presence, the outdoor air, even the cigarette smoke was calming. I found a whale in the clouds, a sailboat, an evil clown.

The grass rustled, and Leo rolled onto his side. I did the same and faced him. I marveled at being this close to him, finding freckles on his nose, watching the way the sunlight made his red eyelashes almost transparent. Then out of nowhere he kissed me. It was a hard kiss, a quick one. Then he pulled back and took a drag off his cigarette, turning his head to blow the smoke away from my face.

"Why'd you do that?" I asked, hiding the smile and desire that seeped from every pore in my body.

"You looked like you wanted me to," he explained, then took another drag.

"What does that mean?" I asked, annoyed. "Was I pursing my lips? Were my tits glowing? What?" He actually laughed loudly at that one. "I'm glad my glowing tits amuse you," I told him.

"They sound very amusing. Mind if I take a look?" he joked. I think.

"Only if you show me your balls of fire," I deadpanned.

He fell onto his back again and looked up at the passing clouds. The sun was starting to set. Summer was definitely over. My dad was gone. My best friend had cancer. And there I was, sharing cigarettes with the boy of my sick and twisted dreams.

That kiss made me feel lit up like his cigarette. Did he want me to kiss him again? Or was that a pity kiss? Was I someone worth pity? How would he even know if I was or not?

I was tired of thinking, so I propped myself up on my elbow and looked down at his mouth. Did it want to be kissed, too? There was only one way to find out, and I went for it. That time the kiss was longer, stronger, and wetter. I fell onto him, not worried at all about my insignificant weight on his substantial chest. He wrapped his hands around my back, then moved down until he squeezed my butt. It felt so good and comforting, I would have been willing to take all of my clothes off right then and there. In that moment, I understood every reason Becca did what she did last summer with Davis.

And then my phone rang. My mom's ringtone. Quite possibly the least sexy ringtone I could have asked for, not that I would have asked for any.

I jerked away from Leo to answer. I hung up. "Hi, Mom. Just driving around. Yeah, I can come home now. See you soon.

"I have to go." I turned to Leo, who perched himself up on his elbow.

"Yeah, okay."

I looked around to find my car keys and stood up. Leo remained in his reclined position while he pulled his cigarettes out of his jacket again.

"So, I guess I'll see you in school," I said. My mind had moved on to what would transpire when I got home, having to tell my mom about Becca.

"Yep." He lit his next cigarette and returned to his back.

Confused but preoccupied, I left him in the grass and drove toward home as though what just happened was as imaginary as a clown in the clouds.

CHAPTER

WHEN I ARRIVED HOME, the house was in a much more chaotic condition than when I had left. AJ and CJ marked their presence everywhere, from their cleats strewn across the doormat to the clots of dirt that made a trail to the basement, where they played an incredibly loud video game. Their stench was also noticeable.

My mom was in the kitchen unpacking some Target bags. "Hi, Mom," I greeted her.

"Hi, honey. How was your day?" she asked as she added to her collection of overpriced hand soaps under the sink.

"It was okay. I guess." Since my dad's death, I hated to burden my mom with anything heavy. But if I didn't tell her about Becca and she somehow found out, then we'd have a blow-up argument about how I don't confide in her anymore. That already happened over the summer when I hadn't told her about me and Becca's friendship hiatus. "Not really, actually. Can I tell you something?"

My mom was still distracted by her unpacking, so I emphasized my need for undivided attention by taking a soap pump out of her hands.

"Honey, what is it?" She sounded concerned, if not exhausted. Mom was a few inches taller than me, which I appreciated for its momness. I looked up at her eyes, dark brown like mine, and said, "I found out today that Becca has cancer."

"Oh, sweetheart. Oh." Mom engulfed me in her arms. I wished she hadn't. I choked, and tears started streaming down my face. By the time I was finished, my mom's shoulder was covered in saltwater and snot. She put her hands on my cheeks after subtly wiping tears from her own eyes. "Do you know anything more? What kind? What stage?"

It seemed ironic, using the word "stage" for cancer and Becca. I knew it wasn't the same meaning, but Becca loved the stage. Whatever stage of cancer she had, I hoped it was a good one. "Hodgkin's lymphoma. I don't know what stage."

"Hodgkin's. That's a good one to have, if there is a good one. Your uncle Alan had it and beat it. Becca's strong like you. She'll beat it, too."

"I hope," I sniffed. "We cut her hair off today."

"That glorious hair. It'll grow back. You know that already. You know so much already." Mom looked at me sadly, and I knew she was referring to my dad.

I didn't want her to get on that morose path, so I said, "She starts chemo tomorrow. I'm going to send her a message to wish her luck."

"You're a good friend." She tried to smile. "I'm so sorry, honey."

"Don't make me cry again, Mom, or I'll rub my boogers all over your other shoulder."

"Then I'll have a matching set." She tried to laugh.

I walked upstairs to my bedroom and shut the door. My over-head light was too bright for my mood, so I turned on my three pop-can lamps from junior high shop class. Each one illuminated a different color: a red bulb from the Strawberry Crush, a green bulb from the Mountain Dew, and a purple bulb from the Shasta. I walked over and drew my shades, then smiled at the memory of Becca flashing her neighbor. I thought about doing it myself, but my bedroom window opened to our backyard and the people in the house behind us were an elderly couple with three ratty poodles. Even if I did flash them, I didn't know if they would still be awake at eight o'clock to see me.

While my computer booted up, I looked at the poster above my head: a Portuguese *Dead Alive* movie poster that read, *Mi Madre se ha comida su perro*, that I bought at the Dead of Winter horror movie convention last year. Would Becca be able to go again when it came to town this winter?

I planned on sending Becca an email, in case she was sleeping and the buzz from a text woke her, but I saw her name in my messaging list.

You awake? I typed.

I waited for an answer, but got none. I typed on anyway.

Maybe you're asleep. I hope you're dreaming aboard Battlestar Galactica.
Weird true story: I saw Leo at the park. Tried a cigarette! Tasted like ass. Then, no shit, we made out. I think I may have imagined it. Wish you were there. Not to watch us, just to verify it happened.

I waited again for a reply. Nothing. She must have left her messenger on.

Well, good night then. Don't let the bed bugs bite. Good luck tomorrow.

I stepped away from the computer to put on my nightshirt, which was really just a t-shirt that had become too holey and yellowed in the armpits to wear in public.

The familiar chime of a message alerted from the computer. On my screen was a message from Becca:

You just did something off my Fuck-It List! I forgot which number. So the question is: Did his mouth taste like ass, too?

I fished the Fuck-It List out of my crumpled jeans on the floor. There at number 12: Kiss a boy who smokes.

I typed back, **Not like ass. Like a burnt hamburger. But a sexy burnt hamburger.**

Goodnight, Alex.

Goodnight, Becca.

I got into bed with the Fuck-It List and crossed out number 12. Something about that action, the dragging of the pen over Becca's words, made me feel like I was helping her. I couldn't cure her cancer, but there were things I could do. And if they happened to be with a guy who I kind of liked, I shouldn't feel guilty about it. After all, it's what Becca wanted.

CHAPTER

10

THAT NIGHT I SPENT over an hour reading over Becca's Fuck-It List. It was like a window into her tween-through-present-day soul. I had no idea about some of her dreams, like number 7: Eat a hot pepper. How tiny. How insignificant. And yet, it must have seemed like a big enough deal to put it on her list. Was that one I would complete for her? Or did she want the easy ones to do on her own?

Number 4: Write Rupert Grint a love letter.

I remembered Becca's Rupert Grint phase, after we first saw *Harry Potter and the Goblet of Fire* on DVD. "He looks so different. So kind of manly." I was a Seamus Finnigan gal myself, but I could understand the appeal of Rupe. I mean, the guy's last name was Grint, and I was no stranger to the admiration of a redhead.

Did Becca actually want me to write him a letter? I wished we had gone over some ground rules. Which ones were more important to her, which she wanted to do herself, and which were so outdated that they could be taken off the list altogether?

What about number 1: Have a Kool-Aid stand with every Kool-Aid flavor invented.

How did that make it to her Fuck-It List? Was it a dying-of-cancer priority? And what kind of asshole would I look like if I did set up a rainbow-flavored Kool-Aid stand?

As the list grew, it also matured in content, hence the neighbor flashing and the smoker kissing. Toward the end, practically every item was about sex or drugs. Number 16: Smoke pot with a burnout behind the school. And number 17: Make out with a burnout behind the school.

I knew which burnout she had in mind, too. Chad Dominguez, her lust-from-a-distance delinquent that fulfilled her bad-boy movie requirements (remedial classes, multiple suspensions, held back at least one grade, and completely edible). Did that mean I had to smoke pot and make out with Chad Dominguez? Would Becca appreciate that I fulfilled items like that or be livid with betrayal? Did Becca have her own copy of the list for reference? What if I lost the list? I vowed to scan the paper first thing in the morning, email Becca a copy, and save one to my hard drive. The paper was already in slightly disintegrated condition; I would hate to fail Becca by accidentally getting it wet or leaving it somewhere. During sleep, I decided to store it under a tall stack of books on my nightstand. I have always kept a stack of library books next to my bed as a lifeline. If I ever woke up in the middle of the night too scared to move or too sad to roll over, the books were my saviors. I picked up an aged copy of Stephen King's *Thinner*. Not his best, but I liked it enough to read it for the third or fourth time. Three pages in, I fell asleep.

The next morning, a half hour before my alarm was set to begin the monotony of the day, and half asleep to where I was still dreamy,

I remembered my time with Leo on the grass. Even if he was only kissing me back because he thought I wanted to kiss him, I could feel he enjoyed it. Both from the hand on my ass and the stiffness in his pants. In my bed, I inched my hand down my stomach and into the band of my underwear. I relived the feeling of my body on top of Leo's, and I rubbed my fingers between my legs, gently at first, just one finger in a circle. As Leo kissed me deeper, pressed against me harder, I added more fingers, my whole palm, faster, urgently until my entire body shuddered.

I lay still, my hand still in my undies, my heart beating heavily. Then my eyes popped open, and my hand ejected itself from the hot seat.

Becca had cancer, and I just fucked myself.

Guilt consumed me, as it had since the moment I learned of her fate just the day before. The day before. Was that how long it had been? Not even really a day? And it was just the beginning. Today was Becca's first day of treatment. She could be in the hospital for days. She could feel sick for weeks. She could even . . .

No. What's that bullshit people love to spout? The power of positive thinking. It couldn't hurt, could it? Not as much as the pain Becca was about to go through, was probably going through already. If she can endure having every cell in her body attacked, then I could make the effort to be a more positive person.

Fuck.

I rolled over and looked at my alarm clock. Two minutes until the radio turned on to the only station that came in with the weak, dangly antenna: Lite FM. It always ensured I got my ass out of bed pronto lest I had to listen to Maroon 5 torment me with their mediocrity.

Underneath the library book stack, I spied the crinkly edge of Becca's list. I gingerly pulled it out so as not to knock over the tower of books or rip the delicate paper. I grabbed a pen from the night-stand, skimmed the list, and found what I was looking for. Number 11: Masturbate.

Even though she wanted to do it, which now meant for me to do it, I still felt guilty. Reluctantly, I crossed it off just as the dulcet vocals of a recently tattooed male assaulted my ears. "Why?" I yelled at my alarm clock, and shut it off. I whipped off my covers and headed straight to my computer.

While the computer booted up, I placed the list into my scanner, a birthday present last year when I was experimenting with Photo-shopping old family photos. My personal favorite was one where I airbrushed my parents to look young and added wrinkles, jowls, and hunched backs to me and my brothers. I called it "Ye Olde Family Portrait." It won second place in the county's high school art compe-tition. What I really hoped for someday was to win an award for my films. If I could ever actually finish one. I was really close at the end of the last school year. I thought I might have a shot at this local film contest hosted by a teen center two towns over. But then my dad died, and I couldn't look at the movie again. Deleted the whole thing from my hard drive. Which was fucking stupid, since it starred Becca and now Becca might not be around forever and I could have had all that footage to remember her and . . .

My mind spiraled to a dark place until I realized my computer was ready for me. I scanned the list, saved it as F-IT LIST, which I thought looked kind of funny. I took out the hyphen. The FIT LIST. As if I were creating some sort of exercise goals list and sharing them with my friends. I opened my email account and saw I had one new message from something called CaringBridge. I thought it might be junk, but I clicked anyway. Completely unjunk, it turned out to be a link to an online cancer journal set up by Becca's mom. I clicked the link, which required me to set up a password, and I read the first entry. It was short, just a few sentences, and read, "We begin treatment today. Becca, newly bald, looks beautiful with or without hair. She is in decent sprits, saying this is perfect research for a future movie role. If only that's all it were."

I pictured Becca's mom typing in a hospital seat, the same kind I had sat in while awaiting the verdict on my dad's life. So kind of hospitals to provide Wi-Fi. I meant that, too. Nothing like the inanity of the web to take one's mind off the stench of pain and death that resides in hospitals.

Positive thinking, Alex.

I opened a new email, subject: **The FIT LIST.**

Becca,

I hope your morning isn't sucking so far. I'm sure it is, and I hope it's not annoying that I'm wishing it wasn't. What the hell am I saying?

Note the attached list. I hope you enjoy the exercise-motivated abbreviation. I also hope you don't leave it open by accident on your computer. You, my dear, are a perv. I hope you will be happy to know I completed number 11 for you this morning. I will gladly complete it for you multiple times a week and whenever I manage to take a bath. I have to ask: Was that an old item that you never bothered to cross off, or have you seriously never diddled yourself? Ew. I just grossed myself out a little with the word "diddle." I hope it's not some weird Jewish guilt thing. Does that exist? Anyway, the deed is done and done well. Have you really never masturbated? I'll tell you a secret, but only because you have cancer (thought I'd remind you in case you forgot): I have only had an orgasm by myself. I don't know why. Maybe I haven't been attracted enough to the guys I've screwed around with. Or maybe they all sucked in the sexual abilities department. (Don't even try to convince me otherwise of Davis. That douche needed to cut his nails.) So maybe I need to start my own Fuck-It List. Number 1: Have an orgasm with an actual guy. Or I could just add it to your list, right after number 20: Go to school dressed like a prostitute. Seriously, Becca, you are a genuine grade-A perv. Only one of the million reasons I love you. Stay strong, my friend.

Time to go to school and pretend I give a shit.

Love,
Alex

After my shower, I dressed myself in my *Dead Set* uniform of black t-shirt, jeans rolled up once, black high-top Chucks, and my low ponytail, and got in my dad's car. Just as I was about to pull out of my driveway, I remembered the list resting in my scanner. It was cleaning-lady day, and who knew how nosy Paulina was when she cleaned my room? I shut off my engine, pounded up the stairs, and pulled out the note. Not wanting to leave it behind, I folded and stuffed it in my front pocket for safekeeping. A quick good-bye to my mom and brothers, who could barely manage a word through shovels of cereal, and I was on my way to school, the lump of the list a constant reminder of my best friend and her lumps.

CHAPTER

11

THE SCHOOL DAY PASSED in a muddy blur. The only class that was interesting enough to help me forget about what I wished I didn't have to forget about was English. My teacher, Ms. Norton, was a spark plug filled with energy and information. She loved the shit out of books, which I couldn't say for all of my English teachers. Some of them liked to analyze a book to death—suck all the truth and light out of a character until they were just inanimate, dissected letters on a page. We went over the year's reading list, and I vaguely listened.

The only interaction I had with Leo that day was through the tiny glass window of the heavy metal hallway doors. We made eye contact, but I lost him in the shuffle of the passing period. Fine with me. Now that we'd actually talked, and then some, I didn't even know what I wanted to say, or do, with him.

At lunch I checked my email in the library. Nothing new from Becca or her mom's journal. I dug around online to see if I could learn anything specific about Becca's treatment, but Google gave me billions of hits and I didn't know what I was looking for anyway. According to Becca, treatments and drugs are tailored to each patient, so even if I did read something it might have nothing to do with what Becca was going through.

All my searching really did was make me puddle-on-the-floor depressed. Not only was my best friend going through this, but millions of other people's best friends, moms, dads, sisters, brothers, *fuck*, even cats were going through it. I looked up at the ceiling and asked, "WHY?" I didn't know who I was talking to. After my dad was killed, I pretty much gave up all belief in God. People loved to say "comforting" things to me, like, "It's part of God's plan" or "God only gives you what you can handle." Um, fuck you? And fuck God. Seriously, if the god they believed in was giving out dead dads and cancer, I wanted nothing to do with him. And yeah, of course I can handle what was doled out to me. Because I was forced to. What were my options? Not handling it? Even that would be a choice and, therefore, the way I handled the situation.

It's pretty damn hard to believe in God when you've lost so much. I know some people go the opposite way. God can be a great being to lean on, like a falling star to make all your superstitious wishes come true. But no matter how long or hard I prayed, I knew my dad would never come back. So why bother?

Still, as I stood up from my chair in the library, I mumbled, "Not her, too." If there was a god, an all-seeing, all-hearing and -knowing superpower of a god, then he'd hear me and know what I was talking about. Not that he'd do anything about it.

After school, I drove to my job at Cellar Subs, a local institution loved by college students and the monetarily impaired. I was the only high school student who worked there, and I got the job after recommending *Dead Alive* to the owner. He went home and watched it the night of the interview, obviously wowed by my taste, and hired me the next day. The college students I worked with were a mix of art majors, lesbians, and frat boys. As much as I loved living here, what with the excellent public library system and the selection of old-timey movie theaters, I would never stay here to go to college. Or, at least, I wouldn't have before my dad died. Now I couldn't even think about college, about leaving. Mom needed me here, and I didn't want to spend my year writing sob-story college applications. The new plan was to save up some money, maybe travel, and figure it out when I was ready. Becca's cancer solidified my idea. Mom didn't push. Maybe she wanted me around, too.

Being at work, where the college students always got to choose the music (that day was a totally weird band called Ween) and the business was always steady, turned out not to be so bad. The rhythmic slap of meat on bread put me at ease, so much so that it took several times of Leo calling, "Alex!" for me to recognize someone was talking to me. I wiped my meaty hands on the rag tucked into my shorts and old t-shirt, rotated from my sleep-shirt collection, and walked out of the kitchen. The restaurant was organized with the front counter at the bottom of the entrance stairway (because, naturally, the restaurant was in a cellar). Above the counter was a menu sloppily written in chalk. When people ordered they were given a number, and their hand-written ticket was passed back to me and my cohort, Doug, a kind of cute, definitely annoying sculpture major with a minor in astronomy. After one of us made the subs, usually me unless we were busy enough to warrant Doug to stop sketching and start sandwich making, we placed it in a basket, left the small, narrow kitchen behind the counter, and yelled out the customer's number. Sometimes I liked to do it in an accent. Today, I just did it as loudly as I could.

Leo waited by the counter, ready to pick up an order.

"Hey," I greeted him with confusion. "How did you know I worked here?"

"I didn't. I always come here on Wednesdays after my tuba lesson."

"You play the tuba?"

"No. I just thought it sounded funny."

"So you're stalking me?" I checked.

"Sorry, no. I actually come here after I pick up my comic subscriptions."

"For real this time?"

"For real."

"The tuba was cooler."

"Says you."

I ignored the annoyed looks of the college students around me, pretending I was oblivious to the fact that they wanted to eat.

"What number are you?" I nodded toward Leo's order ticket.

"Forty-two."

"The meaning of life, no less. I'll be right back."

I went into the kitchen and fixed Leo's order, a veggie deluxe with cheddar and Muenster cheeses heated up. I popped the sub into the microwave above my head and prepared myself the Alex Special: turkey and Muenster, topped with a pile of pickles. When the microwave beeped, most definitely emitting heaps of radiation so near my brain, I informed Doug, "I'm taking my dinner. You have orders to make." I didn't wait around to see if he heard me, tossed my rag onto an empty counter, and carried out the two baskets to Leo.

"Lead the way," he directed. I took him to my favorite spot next to a fake fireplace. Cellar Subs' walls were covered in graffiti, one of those places that encourages it. I left my mark one night after closing, high on the wall so as not to be written over, standing on a ladder from the back room: "Belial was here," a nod to the Basket Case Trilogy.

When we began eating, Leo said, "My compliments to the chef."

"Mine, too," I agreed. "So you really didn't know I worked here?" I asked.

"Did you know I played basketball over at Irving?"

"Nope."

"Then I didn't know you worked here."

"That kind of makes it sound like you did know I worked here, but that I was lying about knowing you played basketball at Irving. Which I wasn't."

"Pickles?" he questioned.

"Want one?" I offered.

"I'm good."

We ate our subs, not breaking for more confusing chat until Leo, wiping his mouth on a tiny, useless napkin, asked, "Should I try a conversation starter?"

I liked the way Leo talked. It wasn't as matter of fact as the way I spoke, but it wasn't as forced as most people would be when getting to know someone. "Do you have one?" I asked.

"That was pretty much it."

"And look at the conversation it started." He shrugged. "I've got one," I said. "My dad made it up. It's called half and half. Like, half empty, half full. You're supposed to say something that happened today that was half empty, you know, shitty? And then something half full, the good." I waited for him to make fun of the quaintness, but he took a thoughtful pause and asked, "Can you go first? I need a minute to think."

"Don't think while I'm talking because then you're not listening."

"Thanks, Mom."

I flipped him off pleasantly and said, "I'm getting drinks. You think about your half and half while I get us pop. What do you want?"

"Coke."

I walked behind the counter to the drink fountain. Ila, a gorgeous women's studies major with waist-length strawberry-blond hair, worked the register. "Who's that?" She waggled her eyebrows at me. I could've been jealous at the thought of not only a college girl, but a beautiful one at that, ogling Leo, but Ila was a lesbian with the cutest girlfriend who, when not going to school full-time, worked as a carpenter.

"That's Leo. From my school."

"Is he your boyfriend?" she asked, completely ignoring the backup of customers. Part of the charm of Cellar.

"No. I don't think so. I don't know what he is. I barely know him, really." I pumped the pop out of the fountain into two worn, plastic tumblers.

"But you want to know him, right?" Ila was overdoing the innuendo, but I liked the big-sisterly vibe.

"Yes. But I don't know. We'll see. Shit doesn't seem to work out very well for me lately. Or ever."

"Hopefully this isn't shit then." Ila started taking orders again, and I delivered our drinks.

"Thanks," Leo said. "I thought of my halves, unless you want to go first."

"After you."

"My half empty is that my brother is still in Sangin, and my parents are constantly terrified. We don't know when he's coming home. And my mom has these screaming nightmares about it."

"That *is* half empty. Are you close with your brother?"

"Yeah. I mean, he's kind of the favorite in the family. My parents worship him. He's annoyingly perfect. And I'm the family fuckup."

"You don't seem like such a fuckup." I sipped my Coke through the straw.

"You must have heard some things."

"Yeah, but not from you."

"Probably everything you heard was true."

"So you slept with Mrs. Johansen, the chorus teacher with the lazy eye?" I asked agape.

"No," he blurted.

"You've been to jail?"

"No."

"You have a tattoo on your ass that reads, 'Kiss this'?"

"Are you kidding me? Who said that?"

"I just made that up. But that would've been awesome if you did."

"Maybe you can give it to me."

"What do you mean?" I smiled over the straw at the insinuation that I could give him a tattoo.

"Don't you have a homemade one?"

"How did you know that?" I could barely contain the rush of Leo Dietz knowing a private factoid about me.

"I saw it once during gym class."

The fact that Leo had watched my thigh at some point during gym class almost made me blush. "Anyway, so what rumors about you are true? Have you really been suspended?"

"I was suspended last year for busting out Daniel Lum's teeth. Even though I didn't really mean to do it. Whatever, the guy's dad's a dentist," Leo mumbled.

"What else?" I pulsed the Coke through the straw in anticipation.

"I was also suspended for having a 'weapon'"—he finger-quoted—"in my locker, which was bullshit because it was a pocket-knife. Boy Scouts are allowed to have them."

"Are you a Boy Scout?" I asked.

"What do you think?"

"How old are you?" I prodded. The rumor was that he was really twenty after being held back twice.

"Twenty-six," he answered. I coughed on my Coke, until he said, "Really? You believed that?"

"What? I don't know you. I mean, for all you know about me, I could be a serial killer."

"I'm counting on it." He smirked. Melt. "And I'm only seventeen."

"So you weren't held back?"

"I was, actually, after we moved. Behavior crap. But I had skipped kindergarten because I was so ahead of everyone. So it all balanced out." We both nodded, and he said, "What about you?"

"I'm seventeen. No skipping or going back."

"I meant your half empty."

"Oh yeah." I wasn't sure what to say, if I wanted to get into Becca's cancer. But he was honest with me, and I didn't have to go into great detail. Not that I had many details. "My half empty is that my best friend has cancer. And she started treatment today, and I don't know what's going to happen or if she'll live or die or when I get to see her or talk to her or if she'll live or die and I know I just said that—"

I nervously lifted my straw in and out of my cup, willing myself to hold it together.

"Jesus, Alex, I had no idea. That sucks. That's like glass almost completely empty. Shit. I thought you were going to say something about your dad, but, damn. I don't really know what to say. Sorry is such a loaded word."

"Thank you for not saying that."

"Alex!" Doug yelled from the kitchen. "Get your ass back in here! I have to take a piss!"

"Fine dining, it is not," I noted to Leo.

We stood up and took our baskets to the garbage. "I guess it's just half empty today." I frowned.

"I'll do my half full really quickly. I got to have dinner with you. And I got a free drink, too."

"You can pay me when I give you your ass tattoo," I told him dryly. I dumped the contents of my basket into the garbage and gave a little wave to Leo. "Have a good night," I said, feeling awkward that I didn't know quite how to say good-bye. I didn't have to know. Leo held my face in his oversize hands and pressed his lips to mine. He was such a good, powerful kisser, I involuntarily hummed with pleasure as I kissed him back, standing on tiptoes as he leaned down to meet me. I gripped the front of his t-shirt with a tight fist to steady myself. The kiss wasn't long, but it was enough to make me wobble back to my spot in the kitchen after Leo uttered, "Good-bye, pickle breath."

I think I found my half full.

CHAPTER

12

I ARRIVED HOME from work around nine thirty. Cellar Subs closed at nine, and it was my job to mop the floor with a seventy-five-year-old mop that weighed 600 pounds. I don't know if the floor ever actually got clean because the lighting was so bad at the restaurant, and the mop was so decrepit. Strings of meat and vegetables slid between the dreadlocks of the mop, long past the expiration of the five-second rule. It was also my job to clean the bathrooms, but nobody actually did that. Cellar had infamously nasty bathrooms, which somehow made the place cooler. Unless you had to use them.

When I walked into my house, AJ and CJ were watching *Wipeout* and laughing uncontrollably at the big balls. I wished I had the ability to be as ridiculously airheady as they did. Not that they were stupid, but as seventh-grade boys they didn't yet feel the weight of the world on their shoulders. Or in my case, my pocket. The only thing I had to show for Becca's list was self-pleasuring before breakfast, and

I didn't even know if she knew about that yet. We hadn't talked about due dates or expectations of numbers. The list was as vague and overwhelming as the cancer itself.

"You smell like a sandwich," AJ told me without looking away from the watery carnage on the TV screen.

"OOOH!" AJ and CJ practiced synchronized cringing at the TV.

"Here." I threw a bag containing two subs to CJ, who dexterously caught it without turning his head.

"Thanks, sis."

"No prob, bros."

I walked into the kitchen for a glass of water. I did smell very sandwichy. It wasn't so bad compared to my first job as an ice-cream scooper. Ice cream may be delicious when you eat it, but it rots when stuck to your shirt. Washing it never got the rank smell out either. The sandwich smell did come out of my clothes, but sometimes it took forever to excrete from my nose.

I pulled the blue Brita pitcher out of the fridge and poured myself a tall glass of water. I placed the pitcher back, and my eyes focused on a jar that I never paid much attention to: jalapeño peppers, which my brothers ate for sport. They never appealed to me. Food and pain together seemed like a weird combo.

"AJ. CJ. Come here," I called into the other room. I pulled out the Fuck-It List from my pocket, and as I remembered, number 7, an early one, read: Eat a hot pepper. Great. Couldn't I just have sex with a member of the chess team or something?

"We're watching *Wipeout*!" they chimed in unison.

"Pause your big balls and get in here!" I demanded.

The clumsy shuffling of my twin brothers arrived in the kitchen.

"What?" CJ held his sandwich in the brown paper bag like some drunk on the street. He took a sandwich swig and chewed lazily.

"What's it like to eat a hot pepper?"

"What do you mean? You just stick it in your mouth and bite it," AJ explained helpfully.

"That's what she said," CJ chuckled.

"Are you guys really this corroded?" I glared.

"No, sorry. You did bring us sandwiches," AJ conceded.

"I wanted to try an experiment." There was no way I'd tell my brothers about the Fuck-It List. "But I'm a little scared."

"You can watch *The Texas Chainsaw Massacre*, but you can't eat a pepper?" CJ asked. He couldn't stand horror films, especially after Dad died. It was kind of sad and sweet at the same time. One of the traits that made him slightly human. Plus, it was fun watching him run away from the TV when I had a movie on in the family room.

"Those movies aren't real. Well, actually, *The Texas Chainsaw Massacre* was based on a true story," I explained.

"Don't tell me that!" CJ covered his ears, one with a hand and the other with the sandwich in a bag.

"Dudes, help me here. I have to eat one, and I just want to prepare myself."

AJ walked over to the jar I pulled from the fridge. "This one's for pussies. You have to try ghost chiles instead. They'll burn your butthole for days."

"I don't eat with my butthole." I eyed them.

"Yeah, but they have to come out after you digest them. They're the gift that keeps on giving. Burn you in, burn you out." AJ nodded in a sick way.

"You guys are freaks," I told them.

"We'll eat one if you do," CJ volunteered. "For twenty bucks," he added.

"You'll do it because I'm your sister and you love me, and if you don't I'll put my Chuckie doll in your bed in the middle of the night." Chuckie was an evilly-stitched doll from the movie *Child's Play*. Not the best movie, but I found the doll at a horror con in great condition and couldn't pass it up. "Plus: sandwiches."

"Fine. But you get to apologize to my butthole in the morning."

"I'll notarize a letter and everything. Let's do this."

CJ unscrewed the jar lid and a tangy smell tickled my nose. "You don't have any cuts on your fingers, do you?" I examined my hands and shook my head no. "Good." He carefully pinched his thumb and forefinger around a bright green pepper and pulled it out of the jar. He slid the jar over to me, and I did the same. Juice dripped off the pepper onto the kitchen table, and I half expected a hole to sizzle into the wood.

"On the count of three?" I asked. CJ nodded. "One. Two. Three." I closed my eyes and bit the pepper from its stem. It didn't immediately hurt, but a slow sting emanated throughout my mouth. My eyes watered, and so did my nose. My lips felt about six sizes bigger than usual. When I finally managed to swallow, I coughed and sneezed simultaneously.

"Water!" I choked and chugged my entire glass. That didn't help. AJ and CJ were in hysterics, leaning on each other for support. "You didn't eat it, did you?" I guessed.

"No. But thanks for the kind offer," CJ said.

I rubbed tears from my eyes. "No problem. And Chuckie can't wait to see you."

"No! I'll eat it! Watch!" He stuffed it into his gaping mouth.

"Too late." I poured myself a second glass of water, not waiting to see CJ's reaction before I walked up the stairs to my room.

"I ate it! Al, I ate it!" He sputtered after me.

"Chuckie can't hear you anymore," I cackled, and shut my bedroom door.

While my computer revved up, I crossed off number 7. "Only for you, Becca," I said to the paper. A hot pepper, as painful as it was, was still an easy item. If I were to accomplish any of the big-ticket numbers, like Take a bath in someone else's house, that would take some planning. Same with number 10: Hop a train like a hobo. I laughed out loud at that one, not only because the word "hobo" was hilarious, but that Becca would consider such an act worthy of a life-defining list. And what about the last item on the list, number 23: Have sex with someone I'm in love with and who's in love with me. It's not something I'd ever accomplished before, so how easy could it be now that it was with a time limit? I'd only actually had sex with one person, but I didn't even believe I was in love with him at the time. His name was Aleks, pronounced the same as my name and short for Aleksander, an exchange student from Norway who stayed with our next-door neighbors. It was last fall, after Thanksgiving but before winter break. There were fifteen Norwegians in total imported to our school, and Aleks didn't look much different from the rest of them: tall, sandy blond hair, solid, round head. They traveled in packs, laughed loudly, and spoke a language that sounded both fluid and funny. Before I had a car, I took the bus to school. So did Aleks, along with Katie Cartwright, the neighbor he stayed with who was a grade younger and a zombie cheerleader. Katie and Aleks never sat near each other on the bus, nor did I ever see them exchange words. Aleks sat by himself near the front, until the other Norwegians boarded a few stops later. Then he lit up and became animated. I liked to watch them, imagining someday that I might become an exchange student or live in another country. It was a dream that I tried not to hang on to anymore for fear that an unrealized dream would make me realize just how stranded I was now that my dad was dead.

One afternoon, when Aleks and I got off the bus alone, Katie at a game or something, he asked in a lightly clipped accent, "Want to come over?"

I had no reason to say no, and I was curious. "Sure." I shrugged. We ended up hanging out in his adopted room, not talking much but watching *The Big Bang Theory* reruns from his bed. Nothing happened the first day, but I sensed he wanted it to.

A week later, sans Katie, he invited me over again. I went more as a spy for Becca, who seemed to think that Norwegians were the sexiest human beings alive and vowed to catch at least a glimpse of one of their uncircumcised penises. Besides, Aleks smelled nice. I had never been one for perfume or cologne and felt downright revulsion for Axe body spray, but Aleks smelled like he cared about his appearance. It was a little salty and minty, as I imagined the water around Norway smelled.

As we lay on his bed, again watching *The Big Bang Theory*, I asked him to teach me some swears in Norwegian.

"Dritsak," he explained, meant "sack of shit." "Hestekuk" meant "horsecock." I laughed that he would think to teach me "horsecock" as a swear, and I swooned a little at the cultural difference. Yes, I swooned at "horsecock."

I wore a button-down shirt that day, and after we laughed about horsecock, Aleks began to unbutton it. We hadn't yet kissed, but he was already taking off my shirt. I let him, curious what this Norwegian would do next. He watched my expression, maybe waiting to see if what he was doing was okay. I assisted him with the many buttons, letting him know it was. When my shirt was completely undone, he kissed me, a little too wet and tonguey. I guided his face down to my chest, and he lightly kissed above, then under my bra. He worked off my shirt, and I sat up enough for him to unhook the back of my bra, which he did adeptly. I guess bra hooks are international. I tugged his gray sweater over his head and ran my fingers up his torso and chest. He was lean and not very muscular. His chest was bare of hair. I remember kissing on the lips very little. He kept his mouth on my breasts most of the time, and I didn't mind. His strong jaw tickled me as he nibbled.

That was as far as it went that day. Katie's pom-poms charged up the stairs about a half hour after we started, and I got dressed and left. Becca was disappointed I hadn't seen his penis yet and handed me a condom the next time I saw her.

Two days later, armed with the Trojan, I followed Aleks back to his house once again. This time the TV stayed off and we immediately began removing each other's clothes when we entered his room. He was qualified at clothing removal but not as much with finger placement. I had to fish his pokey fingers out of my undies twice before he got the hint to give that up.

Me in my underwear, him in his blue boxers, we moved over to the bed. "Wait——" I told him, the first word spoken that afternoon. I found Becca's condom in my backpack and brought it up to the bed. He yanked off his underwear in an overly excited manner, then got on his knees to help me work off mine. I looked at his penis, studying it to get the details for Becca before he slapped on the condom. I lay down on the bed, and he lay on top of me. The initial pain wasn't excruciating, although I never got much pleasure out of it. It was over quickly, and Aleks rolled off me and promptly fell asleep. *Hestekuk.*

I got dressed and immediately called Becca from my cell on the way out of the house. "His penis was wearing a saggy hat," I reported.

"Really? That's so depressing. Did it at least feel good?"

"It felt fine." I shrugged to the phone.

"Well, that's not how sex should feel. Go back in there and do it again!"

"Um, no thank you. Not today at least."

"They go back to Norway next week, you know."

"Well, then we better hurry and have as much bad sex as we can before he leaves."

"Was it really bad?" She pouted over the phone.

"No. Don't worry. It just wasn't really good. I'll try again, maybe. Just for you."

"You're the best."

"Tell that to my vagina."

"You're the best, Alex's vagina."

"My vagina thanks you."

Aleks and I had sex once more before he flew back to Norway. It was better the second time around, with some added foreplay and a near climax. But near isn't the same as the real deal, which was why I wasn't in a hurry to try again when I started dating Davis.

Would the Fuck-It List magically help me fall in love and have sex in a way that I couldn't before Becca got cancer? Was it fair for either of us to live or die with that kind of pressure?

No email from Becca waited on my computer. Her mom sent another report:

The news (not in order of importance):

We will be home Saturday.

Becca will have seven days of chemo in a row, then a two and a half week break, then three to five more treatments followed by a short radiation treatment to zap any remaining tumor cells.

Morphine seems to be working for pain management, and Becca is able to sleep a little, thank God.

After God, she thanked everyone else for being so supportive, but I skimmed that part. It sounded like Becca was in hell, and would be in hell, for a very long time.

I typed Becca an email:

You will be happy to learn that masturbating wasn't the only thing I did on your list. I ate a hot pepper for you. You're welcome. You can thank my burning butt tomorrow morning.

Leo stopped by Cellar. We kissed again. I have no idea what's going on, but he's a really good kisser. Far better than that Norwegian.

Sweet, circumcised dreams, my friend.

CHAPTER

13

JENNA BROWN CAUGHT MY EYE during the morning hallway rush and gave me a sympathetic actorly smile. I threw up a middle finger and scratched my cheek with it, but she was already off and running with her audience. At lunch I decided to join the living and ate with some of my old stage-crew friends. Damien West had shoulder-length black hair and was a practicing Wiccan. He had been hospitalized for depression three times since I'd known him. I think he was just too smart for his parents, and they had no idea what to do with him. His girlfriend, Eliza Klise, was wafer thin and white-out pale with light blond hair she dyed in various colors as it washed out. Currently it was a pukey shade of green. Not her best. Lastly was Brandon Hathaway, tall and thin, with olive skin and rich brown eyes. I was madly in love with him freshman year, even kissed him once, until he came out. I was pissed at him for a while, going far enough to kiss me, but he said he did it because he felt bad for me. Apparently I really looked like I wanted him to kiss me. I wish someone would take a picture of that face so I'd stop making it. Once I got over the humiliation, he was still fun to be around. And he was an excellent judge of character. He advised me heavily against dating Davis, but I didn't listen. Obviously.

"How's our little devil child?" Brandon patted my head as I sat down at the table with a Coke and vending machine packs of cheese and peanut butter crackers. He liked to pretend I was satanic because of my love for horror movies.

"Okay, I guess. You guys heard about Becca?"

"Yeah. How is she?" Damien asked, concerned.

"I don't know yet. I mean, she officially has cancer and is going through chemo and all that. That's pretty much it." I bit into my cheese crackers, while Eliza stared at me. "What?" Bright orange crumbles sprayed from my mouth.

"It's just, how can you eat? At a time like this?"

"Some of us need food to survive," I reminded her.

"Sha, but I don't know, I'd be crying all the time if Damien had cancer. I don't know how I'd make it through the day."

"Alex doesn't cry," Brandon explained. "She's on the spectrum." I sneered at Brandon, and he added, "Maybe just a little bit?"

"I don't know. But why do I have to cry all the time? To prove to you that I'm upset? Fuck that noise. Becca likes to be the dramatic one anyway."

"That's why you guys make such good friends. She's the actress, and you're on the spectrum." Brandon stuck to his brilliant theory.

"I'll shove a spectrum up your ass if you don't stop talking about it."

"Duly noted."

"Is there anything we can do for her?" Damien offered.

"Not that I know of yet. I can ask her."

Changing the subject all too easily, Eliza cattily asked, "Did you hear that Lottie McDaniels is back?"

"The bitch is back," Brandon sang.

Lottie McDaniels was Becca's major competition when she first started in freshman drama, but last year she opted for a boarding school with a stellar acting program. Good riddance. Having her back the same year Becca would be MIA from productions would ensure her superstar status and enlarge her already infamously ginormous head.

"Oh—" I started, remembering something from Becca's list. I unfolded the soft paper from my pocket. "Aha!" I exclaimed.

"What is it, Dr. Watson?" Brandon asked.

"Becca asked me to do some things for her—"

"I thought you said there wasn't anything we could do for her," Eliza whined.

"Simmer down, Doolittle. This is stuff *I* can do for her. Only me. When your best friend gets cancer, then it's your turn." Dramatic sigh from Eliza. I always thought she would have been better on stage than behind it.

Number 14: Tell off Lottie McDaniels.

That should be interesting. I never really spoke to Lottie; she just yelled commands at me during my minuscule stint in stagecraft. Becca told me tales of sabotage, like when Lottie threw out Becca's base makeup because she claimed it smelled weird. I never liked the look of Lottie. There was something messed up about a high school student who wore stiletto heels. How would she run if there was a zombie attack?

The lunch bell rang, and I went on my mission. My lunch friends attempted to push and prod me to tell them what I was reading off of, what Becca wanted me to do. But that list belonged to me and Becca. Plus, they didn't need to see the items I had already checked off. Not that I felt ashamed of any of them, but I didn't need to give out explanations either.

Eliza had gym with Lottie next period, and I found Lottie in the new girls' bathroom outside the small gym. The administration was slowly redoing areas of the school, and a new bathroom meant automatic handles, toilets, and sinks. Soon they'd be pissing and shitting for us, too.

Lottie watched herself in the mirror as she applied a thick layer of reflective gloss to her plump lips. She smacked them together and then, as though I weren't in there to berate her, winked at herself in the mirror. She had almost a foot on me in her heels, but I didn't care. I don't know if I would've cared much before Becca's list, but having a mission and someone to answer to made me even bolder.

"Hey," I said to gain Lottie's attention.

"He-ey," she sang to her own image in the mirror.

"You're Lottie McDaniels, right?" I was 99 percent sure, but revenge was only best served if it was at the right dinner party.

"Of course." She had yet to look at me. I had yet to actually figure out what I wanted to say. Was I supposed to tell her off in the name of Becca? As Becca herself? As just some random Lottie hater? A second bell rang, indicating we were both late for class. I didn't care, since I had art next and for all Mr. Bowles knew, I was working in the darkroom.

"Shit," Lottie said to herself, and stuffed her makeup into her purse. I never understood purses at high school either. Just carry a frakkin' backpack. She brushed past me, as if we hadn't been having a meaningful, "hey"-filled conversation.

"Hey!" I called to her loudly. This time she turned to look at me. Her expression read no recognition. "I have a message from Becca Mason."

"Oh yeah?" She put her hands on her hips and waggled her head like a bobblehead version of herself. "What?"

Obviously, she hadn't been informed of Becca's cancer. Or maybe she was that cold of a skag. Either way, it was my job to tell her off. I said the first thing that came to my mind. "You're a scene-chewing, talentless tart who needs to pull the jeggings out of your camel-toe." I looked pointedly at her too-defined crotch area, then whipped around on my gym-shoed heels and walked out. She clacked after me.

"Becca told you to tell me that?" Her mouth was agape. I saw a gray pile of gum dangling on her tongue.

"Not in those words exactly. I put my own gentle touch on them. Becca would have been more eloquent, but, alas, she's not here right now to talk to you. I hope I made a suitable replacement."

Lottie sputtered and sighed, a look of disgust on her face. "You tell that bitch she'll never make the lead roles this year now that I'm back."

"You can tell her. When she gets done with chemo."

"What?" Lottie's head shrunk back, her eyes opened wide.

"Becca has cancer. She wanted me to tell you you suck, in case she dies and doesn't have the chance to do it herself."

"You're kidding. That's horrible. She said that?"

Sometimes I don't realize how awful I can sound until I see the person's face react to my words. Becca would never have the nerve to say what I did, and even if she did, would she have wanted to?

"You know what? Forget it. I just, like, went off my meds or something."

I began walking away, cursing my social ineptitude. Lottie clacked after me and yanked me around by my arm.

"Does Becca really have cancer?" Her look was genuine concern, not actorly fakeness topped with perfect lip gloss. I shook away her gripping hand, met her eyes, and blankly answered, "Yes."

"Tell her I hope she gets better soon. Tell her"—she considered her words—"there won't be any competition without her."

I gulped. "I will." We stood looking at each other for a minute, until I'd had enough and turned away. "I gotta go," I mumbled, and tripped over my feet, not getting away fast enough.

Apparently I was moving too fast, looking back over my stupid, insensitive, cold-as-ice shoulder, because I slammed right into the chest of Leo Dietz.

CHAPTER
14

I LOOKED UP AT LEO, a tad out of breath.

"Running from some zombies?" he questioned.

"Something like that." I looked down at his shoes, identical to my ratty black Chucks, except for the massive size difference. My expression must have been somewhat telling. Why was it that I never said the appropriate thing, but my face betrayed me and showed off every emotion?

"You okay?" He gently held his knuckle under my chin to raise my head. It was so strangely comforting and annoyingly masculine, I wanted to suck on his fingertips in the middle of the hallway.

"Just put my foot in my mouth. Maybe two feet. I can't do anything right even when I'm trying to do right by someone."

"I don't know what that means. But I'm guessing you probably do a lot of things right." He let go of my chin and stuffed his hand into his army jacket pocket.

"Sometimes it feels like if I really did things right, my dad wouldn't be dead and Becca wouldn't have cancer. I know that's fucking stupid." I cut myself off. I had a lot more to say on the matter, but I'd done enough talking earlier to fill my asshole quotient for the month.

"I don't think it's fucking stupid. I think shit like that all the time. Wrong place, wrong time, wrong person. What if? All that bullshit."

We stood in the hallway, the cloud of my idiocracy hovering over us. "Come with me." He grabbed my hand and pulled me along.

"I can't leave school. I have a quiz in AP History this afternoon," I told Leo.

"So do I. And we're not leaving." He spoke as he dragged me along. I didn't know he took AP History.

"Can you slow down? My stride is about half the length of yours."

"Sorry. I'm trying to get us out of the hallway before a monitor asks us where we're supposed to be."

"Where *are* you supposed to be?"

"Auto shop," he answered, glancing around a corner stealthily, then pulling me along again.

"Hey!" I whisper-yelled. "I'm not a cavegirl."

"Then good thing I didn't club you over the head." He stopped in front of a metal door in the back of a locker section in a yet-to-be-redone part of the school.

"Are you about to take me into a janitor's closet?" I asked.

"Better." He fished a key ring from out of his pocket and flipped through it until he found the one he was looking for.

"Is it the boiler room? Is this the part where we both fall asleep and Freddy comes after us? 'Cause I could so kick his ass."

His key clicked open the lock, and he held open the door. "After you."

I stepped into a small room, maybe ten feet square, piled floor to ceiling with books. A few old student desks balanced precariously in a corner. One naked lightbulb dangled from the ceiling.

"What is this? And why do you have the key?" I asked, sliding into a lone desk chair.

"It's one of the English department storage closets. These are old class sets of books that never get used anymore. I took the key last year out of a teacher's drawer and spent study hall trying doors until I found this place. No one ever comes in here."

I stood up and ran my fingers across the book towers. Classics like *Moby Dick* and *Adventures of Huckleberry Finn* and an array of Shakespeare titles in tiny, hardbound books quivered at my touch.

"So do you want to tell me what you were running from?" Leo leaned against the closed door. He looked almost sinister in the weak, shadowed light, like a man in a dream you're not supposed to talk to but desperately want to touch.

I wondered what my face was saying now.

"Becca gave me something." I cleared my throat, asking myself if I wanted to tell him about the list. He didn't prod, which made me trust him. And he didn't know Becca, which made me feel less guilty about sharing her secrets. Because now they were my secrets, too. "It's a list of things she wants to do before she dies. We call it the Fuck-It List." I laughed nervously, but his stoic expression remained unchanged. "And because she might, maybe, actually die, and she doesn't know if she'll get to do everything on the list, I said I'd help her."

Leo asked, "So, what, like bungee jumping and dropping acid and going on an African safari?"

"Are those things on *your* bucket list?" I cringed a little. They sounded so unoriginal, and I hoped he was beyond that.

"I don't have a bucket list. Nor do I feel the need to pay someone to drop me off a bridge. If I wanted to, I'd do it myself."

"I hear that," I concurred.

"So what, then?" he pressed.

"Just sort of random things that she wanted to do. Some are small, like eating a hot pepper."

"Quite a goal," he said, not exactly sarcastically but definitely unimpressed.

"Fuck you. She started the list when she was nine. And eating a hot pepper isn't that easy."

"Sorry," he said. "What are some of the bigger ones?"

I didn't want to get into it, all of the sexual requests and how Leo helped fulfill more than one of them, with him and by myself. "Well, like today, I was helping her with number fourteen—telling off Lottie McDaniels. Only I fucked it up and was a total cunt and said something about her camel toe." I shook the memory loose from my head.

Leo laughed, a hearty laugh, which pissed me off. "What?" I demanded.

"I just like how you used the words 'cunt' and 'camel toe' in a sentence."

"Oh." We were both quiet, so I pulled a *Tempest* from atop a pile and flipped through the pages. A dried crumble of a page withered in my hands. I returned the book to its deathbed.

"Come here," Leo beckoned. Maybe I was making the face again, or maybe it was the romantic nature of locked rooms and interrogation lighting, but I suspected what came next. At least the first part.

I obeyed Leo and walked up to him at the door. He wrapped his lithe arms around my waist and pulled me against him, leaning forward to meet my lips. We kissed urgently, tongues reaching for each other's, nibbling at one another's lips. I rubbed my hand along the back of his hair, the short pieces tickling my palms and making them tingle. He took his hands off my back, and I felt them wrangling with the button on the front of my jeans.

Were we about to have sex in a book closet? My body would have said yes to anything with Leo at that moment, probably most moments, but my head did the talking. I pulled away from his lips. He switched to kissing my neck, my cheek, my ear. I could hardly speak. "I don't want to have sex right now." When I heard the words, they sounded so unsexy, such a complete passion killer. But they were true. He didn't seem to mind.

Breathing in my ear, he whispered, "We don't have to," and gently bit my earlobe. My legs could barely stand anymore.

We continued to kiss each other anywhere we could reach while he unzipped my jeans. I believed him when he said we didn't have to have sex, so I didn't stop him when he slid his hand into the top of my undies and moved a skilled finger in circles in exactly the right spot. I stopped my kisses and leaned into his soft t-shirt, inhaling his deodorant smell as I tried to command my legs to remain upright. With his free hand, he willed my face toward his again, and we kissed in rhythm with his fingers. I gripped the back of his neck to hold myself up, and his fingers moved faster. This was nothing like the poking of Davis, and I tensed my body as I had done uncountable times alone in my bed. I lost the ability to kiss, to control anything, and I bit his shirt to stop myself from screaming and calling attention to the book closet.

We stood against each other once it was over, still but breathless. The faint sound of the school bell rang outside the metal door. Quietly, Leo said in my ear, "AP History. I have to go." He held me by the side of my arms and gently pressed me away from him. I steadied myself against a small spot of cinderblock wall, zipped and buttoned my jeans.

Before Leo opened the door, he walked over to me and gave me a last gentle kiss on the lips. "Feel better?" All I could manage was a nod.

CHAPTER

15

BECCA WAS NOWHERE to be found online, and my texts weren't returned until Friday morning. According to Becca's mom's report she was home after three days in the hospital and would get oral chemotherapy at home for several days. She wrote that nausea was her worst side effect. I emailed Becca a lite version of the Lottie McDaniels story, focusing more on the nice things Lottie said about Becca rather than the ass-eyed things I managed to say. As I was leaving for school, my phone buzzed. A text from Becca read, "I'm sorry. Just hoarked on Mr. Toad."

Mr. Toad was a stuffed animal I bought for Becca when my family visited Disneyland a few years ago. She had told me how Mr. Toad's Wild Ride terrified her as a kid, so naturally I had to buy the toy.

S'OK. U can borrow my Chuckie doll
LOL
How are u?

Be thankful you cant smell over the phone

When can I see u?

Dunno. Call me after school.

\m/

I left for school with a spring in my step, or at least more springy than my normally springless body was. Becca was alive and well enough to joke-text, and that would get me through the day. I managed to nicely avoid running into Lottie McDaniels when I saw her striking figure in the hallway and turned around, only to knock into Leo again. I smiled at him, and he looked leery.

"Did you poison someone?" he questioned.

"Why? Because I'm smiling? Give me some credit. My assassinations would be much more subtle than that. No, just kind of having a good morning. Are you stalking me again, by the way?"

"Yes. Want to tell me about your morning while you escort me to gym?"

"Wish I could, you know, be your hired escort and all, but I have to get to physics. I need to be awake during attendance so I can nod off during the movie. What about my lunch, your creative writing?" It turned out Leo's creative writing independent study, which only required a check-in before he could head off to "write," was at the same time as my lunch hour.

"Fridays I actually have to talk to my IS sponsor, so I can't do it. Can you miss art?" We talked as we navigated through the shrieking hallway crowd.

"Not today. Critique day."

"Then I guess I'll just see you tonight." We stopped in front of the gym hallway.

"Tonight?" I asked.

"Bruce Campbell. *Army of Darkness* screening? I had an extra ticket." He looked a mixture of annoyed and disappointed that I didn't remember.

"I totally forgot. A lot on my brain, I guess. I can still go." I drummed up some enthusiasm. Not that I wasn't excited, it was just that now Becca was home maybe I should stay by my computer in case she wanted to chat. There was always my phone, though.

"If you're not too busy," he mumbled. Now I could tell he was annoyed.

"Dude. I said I wasn't busy. It just slipped my mind. There's a lot of shit going on, and I just forgot. No big."

"If you say so. Can you drive?" The bell rang.

"Shit. I have to go. I've been late every day since school started."

"People appreciate consistency."

"Teachers aren't people!" I called to him as I sprinted down the hall. "I'll come get you at seven!"

"Make it six. I want to get good seats!"

Ms. Leff didn't seem to notice I was late, and I managed to ask her a question before the movie began to ensure I was accounted for. When the lights dimmed, I texted Becca.

U still puking?

Ten minutes later, still no answer.

Is it ok if I go to a movie with Leo Dietz tonight?

This time, I got a response.

Only if you two sleep on a beach after.

☺

Skype later?

\m/

My mom and the twins sat at the kitchen table when I got home from school. "What's everyone doing?" I asked, and joined them.

"We were just looking through this box of old photos. Remember how your dad was so into Halloween?" Mom smiled sadly at the memory.

"Remember? He was still around last Halloween," I said.

My mom's smile drooped, as did her hand holding the picture. She rose from her chair and left the room.

CJ stood up and shoved my head.

"What the fuck?" I yelled.

"You don't say something like that to Mom."

"Like what? What kind of shitty memory would I have if I couldn't even remember less than a year ago?" I argued.

"It's not about how long ago; it's about the fact that he's not here for *this* Halloween," AJ explained.

There goes my foot-in-mouth disease. I walked out of the kitchen to find Mom slumped on the couch. She wasn't crying, but her expression and eyes were glassy. I sat down next to her, close but not touching.

"Sorry, Mom. I didn't realize what I was saying."

"I know. You never do." She shook her head.

"Um, ouch?" I said.

"Sometimes it would be nice for you to think before you speak. Just in case what you're thinking isn't what everyone else is thinking." Mom looked at me, exhausted.

"I know. It would be easier if everyone *was* thinking what I was thinking, though."

"You'd hate that, Alex," she sniffed with a laugh.

"With a fiery passion from hell," I agreed.

"So what do you have going on tonight? Is Becca home?"

"She is home. I got a couple of texts from her. She said she was really nauseous. I don't know when I'm going to be able to go over there."

"Maybe we can send her a cookie basket."

Mom loved cookie baskets from this place where they make and frost cookies in all different shapes with sappy messages like, "Bee Mine," and "Get Whale Soon." They were pretty tasty, though.

"I bet she'd like that," I said because it felt like what I was supposed to say. What I was actually thinking was: Would Becca even want cookies if she was throwing up all the time? "I'm going to see if she's on Skype. Maybe we can talk before I go out." I pushed myself off the couch.

"I thought you weren't going out," Mom said.

"Oh yeah. Is it okay if I go see Bruce Campbell talk about *Army of Darkness* at the Orpheum? They're showing the movie, too."

"Not by yourself, I hope."

"No, just with someone from school. A guy. Leo Dietz." I paused at the bottom of the stairs, waiting for my mom's reaction.

"Leo? A new boyfriend?" Since Dad's death, Mom wavered between her old, uptight self and trying to fill in for the missing, laid-back parent.

"Not really. Just a guy who likes horror movies." And, you know, other things we can do together. "I'm driving."

I thought maybe my driving would put Mom's mind at ease; the unknown of other kids' driving records sent her into hysterics if I was even a minute late. She seemed to trust me in the driver's seat, since she helped train me. And she knew my seat belt worked.

"What time will you be home?" she asked instead of told me, her attempt at cool.

"The movie starts at eight, so maybe eleven? Twelve? I don't know how long the Q&A will go."

"Call me if you'll be later than eleven thirty."

"Will do," I told her as I left for my room.

Normally, I never kept Skype open because my aunt Judy was like a Skype vampire, waiting to suck away any time I had chatting with her. Once I even deleted her as a contact, but she called my mom within minutes to report it. I had to make up an excuse about accidentally clicking on her name instead of an ex-boyfriend I meant to delete, which would never happen since Skype asks you repeatedly if YOU ARE SURE you want to delete the contact.

For Becca, I opened Skype. Before I had the chance to video call Becca, my computer rang. It was Aunt Judy. If I didn't talk to her, she would call the entire time I was on with Becca. I clicked to answer.

"Hi, Aunt Judy."

"Oh, Alex, so glad to see you! And on a busy Friday night, I'm sure."

"Yep." I nodded casually.

"So, any new boys in your life?"

Aunt Judy seemed to fancy herself the young and hip aunt, which was hard to be when you sported a curly mullet without a hint of irony.

"Aunt Judy, I can't really talk. I have to Skype with my friend.

She has cancer." I hoped just laying it out there would clam the old lady up, but then it turned into a bloated pity fest.

"OH MY GOD! MY POOR ALEXANDRA. WHAT CAN I DO? ARE YOU OKAY? IS SHE OKAY? OH MY GOD!"

"Aunt Judy!" I had to yell several times until she took a break to exhale and grab a tissue from her bra. "I have to go. She's calling me on Skype right now," I lied.

"YOU TAKE CARE OF YOUR—"

I hung up on her. I hoped she'd get the hint to give me space from Skype, but it could also go the way of the concerned check-in, too. I liked Aunt Judy, though. She sent fat checks for birthdays and was actually the first person to show me a horror film when I was eight. My parents had dropped me off at her house for a dinner date, and Aunt Judy put in a tape of one of her favorite childhood movies, *Heidi*, so I could watch while she made dinner. Turned out it was not *Heidi*, but *Carrie*, and by the time Aunt Judy came to tell me dinner was ready, Carrie was being scolded by her psycho mom and getting her period in the shower. Such sweet, innocent times those were.

Becca's icon, a headshot of the gorgeous Number Six Cylon from *Battlestar Galactica*, showed that she was signed on to Skype, but that didn't mean she would answer. I clicked on the video call button and let it ring. No answer.

That gave me time to think about tonight. I didn't want to call it a date, didn't want to think about the attachment and attention and commitment that came with having a boyfriend. I needed all of that for Becca, not some guy I only knew in my dreams until last week. So far it had been easy enough, fun even, and definitely fulfilling in certain areas. That's where I wanted it to stay.

I decided not to change clothes.

In ten minutes, I'd leave to pick Leo up at his house, a house I'd driven by dozens of time with Becca riding shotgun when I first got my license, in hopes of catching a glimpse of him. I liked those glimpses. Nothing serious about a glimpse. I didn't need any more serious.

Just as I was about to leave my room, my Skype rang. I thought it might be Aunt Judy checking in, but happily it was Becca. My view of her was skewed, her laptop on her stomach as she lay awkwardly on her bed with her neck propped up. I forgot for a minute that she had no hair, and her skin was almost chartreuse.

"Hey! How are you?" I asked like a dumbass.

"Gurgle," was all she said, not the sound but the actual word. "I have a puke bucket next to my bed. A bucket of puke," she slurred. I didn't know if she was tired or pumped full of drugs or both.

"Speaking of buckets," I tried to sound cheery, "I've been working on your list. I draw the line at wearing two different shoes, though."

She attempted a smile but could barely hold up her head.

"And I'm going to wait until you're better so we can hop a train like a hobo together."

Was Becca asleep?

"I better let you go. I'm going to see Bruce Campbell tonight with Leo Dietz. Wish it was you, though." Did I really, or did I feel obligated to add that? God, she looked like shit.

After Becca didn't answer, I started to say, "Well, bye. I'll talk to you—"

"Alex. Alex." B came back to life and spoke urgently. "You gotta do something for me," she breathed.

"What? Anything." I meant it, too.

"Find out if he's circumcised." And then she definitely was asleep.

Even sick as fuck and pumped with meds, Becca was a complete pervert. She better not die on me.

CHAPTER

16

LEO WAITED OUTSIDE for me on his front porch. His house had
fancy landscaping with brightly colored window boxes and rounded
bushes. A huge American flag flew from a post.

He slid into my dad's car wearing a pair of jeans spotted with oil
and a dark green t-shirt. I couldn't remember if it was the same outfit
he wore earlier. He smelled minty. "Hey," he said.

"Hey," I agreed, and we drove off.

I had NPR on the radio, a story about Damien Echols, a South-
erner wrongly sent to prison for a sick crime he didn't commit just
because he was an all-black-wearing metalhead and the town needed
a scapegoat. We listened intently, finishing the show as we parked at
the Orpheum. A line snaked around the block.

"Good call on getting here early," I commended him. He placed
his hand on my back to guide me toward the end of the line. It was an
odd feeling. Boyfriendish, almost, and unnecessary. I scooted ahead
of him to find our spot in the queue.

Most of the people waiting were in some kind of costume: fake blood, wigs, one guy even had a disembodied hand gripping onto his shoulder. There was enough people-watching to keep us talking and laughing. I even managed to accomplish one of Becca's early Fuck-It List items—number 3: Chew 10 pieces of gum at once and blow a quadruple bubble. It was rather hilarious to observe Leo as he watched me polish off an entire pack of his Dessert Delight gum. "This apple-pie gum·is fucking gross," I spat through strained chomps of the massive wad in my mouth.

"Not nearly as gross as watching you chew it."

I spat out several double bubbles but never made it close to the coveted quadruple.

At seven, the line began to move, and we made our way to our seats. "Do you mind if we sit on the aisle?" I requested. "I like to have an exit route."

"In case of a zombie attack, I'm assuming." I nodded. Once we were in our seats, Leo asked, "Do you want any snacks?"

"Dots, if they have them," I said, and fished a few dollars out of my pocket.

"That's okay." He wouldn't take the money. "You can pay for coffee later." Leo stood up and rubbed past my knees on his way out of the row. Standing next to him outside in line did nothing for me, but that small act of connecting with my knees made my stomach tingle.

I texted Becca while Leo was away.

About to see Bruce! I'll tell him u say hi

As the lights dimmed for the start of the movie, Leo returned and slid past me once again. I tried to ignore my libido's feelings to retain the reverence of the Evil Dead films. Leo handed me the box of Dots, while he munched from a tub of popcorn. I attempted to remove the clear wrap from around the yellow box in a movie-appropriate manner, but it took me forever to find a weak spot to open the plastic. By the time I was in full crinkle, characters were talking and some people in front of me turned around to glare. I popped a Dot in my mouth and sneered back.

"Ew." I spit the Dot into my hand.

"What's wrong?" Leo leaned over and whispered into my ear. He smelled all buttery.

"I ate a green one," I whispered back. The warmth of his cheek near my mouth begged for a kiss, but I restrained myself.

"Here." He handed me a napkin from under his tub, and I rubbed the sticky mess from my hand into it.

Each time I pulled a new Dot out of the box, I held it up to the screen in hopes of discovering its color in the darkness, lest it be green again.

"Do you want some popcorn?" Leo whispered midway through the film.

"No thank you. Want a Dot?"

"Are there only green ones left?"

"Yep," I told him, and he kissed me one, two, three times on the mouth. I wished there weren't so many people around us.

We watched the rest of the movie as members of an audience, reacting together with laughter and disgust at the appropriate intervals. When the film ended, Bruce Campbell, the lead actor in the Evil Dead trilogy, as well as a cult god, walked out on the stage. He looked paunchier and older than in the films, but still had that great movie star butt chin I admired on him. The audience took several minutes to calm down from our enthusiastic standing ovation, and when we did Leo immediately took my hand in his.

I never was much for holding hands. Most people were so clammy, or our fingers fit together wrong. There was nothing worse than intertwined fingers as a gesture of romance only to realize that the boy's hands were stumpy and there was barely enough room to lace our fingers together. Leo didn't weave our fingers, but held my hand on his lap with a grip that tightened every time he laughed at something brilliant Bruce said. Leo's hand was much larger than mine, with prominent veins. At times, no matter how funny or engaging Bruce was, I was distracted by the force with which Leo would jerk my hand with a laugh. Not a bad distraction, but I wanted to focus on Bruce, maybe learn something for my own movies.

I fished my hand away from Leo's and pretended to dig something out of my back pocket. He didn't seem to notice. I spent the rest of the show wondering why Leo didn't try to hold my hand again.

Bruce was selling and signing copies of his books, posters, shirts, and any other weird artifact people brought to him. When it was time for me and Leo to greet him, I told Bruce, "You are a legend."

He thanked me and offered to sign an *Army of Darkness* poster I brought along. "Gimme some sugar, Baby," he wrote, a classic line. One of my favorites. I asked Leo to take a picture of me and Bruce with my phone, and he did. Then the next person in line, a rather large woman with a *Bubba Ho-Tep* t-shirt on, asked us, "Do you want a picture with both of you?"

"Sure," Leo answered before I could decide for myself. When the moment was over, Leo and I reviewed the picture. We stood on either side of Bruce, smiling like dorks, while Bruce produced bunny ears behind our heads. Classic.

If it were possible for me to feel jubilant, that's how I felt as Leo and I walked back to my car. For two seconds I forgot about my dad and Becca and just reveled in the primo evening.

Leo was bubbly, too, and quoted moments from Bruce's Q&A verbatim. "Remember when . . . ?" "And then he said . . ." It was funny how cute and sweet such a big, supposedly scary guy could look. I started the car, and the clock read 10:45. "What time do you have to be home?" I asked.

"One," he answered.

"Midnight for me. But you can have my glass slipper." He smiled, illuminated by the parking lot lights. "What do you want to do?" I asked. I knew the question was too open, too obvious. At that time of night, we could go back to someone's house and worry about waiting parents, go to Denny's for coffee, which I had previously offered to cover, or find somewhere to park the car.

"How about the Halloween store?" Leo suggested. I hadn't thought of that.

"Is there one up yet?" The phenomenon of pop-up Halloween stores was always exciting and depressing at the same time. Anything huge and Halloweeny meant awesomeness in my book, but they were always thrown into some giant, dead store space that would become empty again once the holiday ended. Or at least until the pop-up Christmas store took its place.

"Sure," I agreed. "Where is it?"

"Where the Borders used to be," he directed.

I drove to the strip mall parking lot and parked in the vast emptiness. We unclicked our seat belts and walked up to the blackened windows. Leo cupped his hands around his eyes and peered in. "I guess we're a little late," Leo noticed as we surveyed the dark store.

"They stay open later when Halloween gets closer," I mentioned.

"Next time," he suggested.

I mulled over the idea of a next time as we returned to the car. "So," I asked as Leo hopped in and shut the door. "What now?" I started the car and turned on WVVX, a local station that turned from Spanish to metal at 8:00 p.m.

As I attempted to tug on my seat belt, Leo slid toward me and ran his hand up my arm. At that moment, the streetlight above the car flickered off. "I planned that," he said. He leaned over and kissed me, his position awkward and sideways, the steering wheel preventing us from getting comfortably close. I gently pushed his chest away from me and crawled my way over the armrest and into the backseat. Leo followed, less gracefully, and stumbled until we were next to each other.

Our hands were everywhere. He pulled my shirt over my head, and I did the same to his. Or was it the other way around? He leaned back onto the leather bench seat, and I rested on top of him. Without taking my bra off, Leo slid his hand inside it and drove me to an embarrassing squeak.

"What was that?" He laughed quietly, as if talking loudly would alert someone outside to our presence.

I bit his lip slightly harder than playfully, which he took to mean I wanted more. I did.

Somehow my hand found its way down to the buttons of Leo's jeans, and I undid them one by one before fitting my hand inside and feeling him against me. He responded with a moan, and dug around until my jeans were unbuttoned, too. We slithered out of our pants and rubbed our barely dressed bodies together, kissing, grinding, gripping. He hooked his finger onto the top of my undies and started to pull them off.

"Wait," I breathed. "We're not going to have sex," I told him.

"Why is it you keep saying that?" He didn't sound annoyed, just curious.

"I've said it twice." His finger remained on my undies, which were now halfway down one side of my leg.

"Does that mean third time's a charm?" He smiled. I smacked his freckled shoulder and shifted onto my knees to pull on my undies. "Wait," he stopped me. "We don't have to have sex. I don't have a condom anyway. Unless you do."

"Even if I did, I said no." My undies were back in place, and I was sitting up. Leo pushed himself up next to me and began kissing my ear.

"Can I still take your panties off if I promise we won't have sex tonight?"

His hands didn't give me time to answer, and he felt so good I wouldn't have said no anyway. After my undies were somewhere on the floor of the car, Leo took my hips and turned me so I was reclining on the seat. He slithered down to where my underwear used to be and placed his hands on either thigh, separating them. I grabbed onto his hair, not hard enough to pull him away from what he was doing but enough to steady myself. Even lying down, I felt like I could fall at any moment. He was masterful at what he did, and I squirmed in painful ecstasy. My head started going to that place where I wondered how he got so skilled, but I willed myself to drown in the moment. I gasped and palmed the car seat, reaching for anything I could before I completely succumbed. When it was over, I released my grip and my hands cramped. I couldn't move. I couldn't talk. I couldn't think. That must be what heaven is like.

I heard Leo groping around for his clothes, and I opened my

eyes. He had a, well, *me*-eating grin on his face, and I was embarrassed to look at him after how I completely let go. When we were both dressed, I noticed the clock. "Shit. I have to get home," I said. We climbed into the front seat, a Megadeth song playing as I drove Leo back to his house. When we got there, Leo unclicked his seat belt. I thought he'd slide over for a good-night kiss, but he just said, "I had a good night."

"Me, too," I answered, rushing home in my head so my mom wasn't worried. I never wanted to call her when I was late, in case she was asleep and my call woke her up. Better to be late without her knowing if at all possible.

There was a pause, both of us wondering what to do. Leo's mom helped us out, calling from the front door. "Leo? Is that you?"

"And that's why we didn't go back to my house," Leo said. "See you Monday." He got out, and I drove away without looking back.

When I got home, Mom was asleep in her room, and the house was quiet.

I went to my room and dug out my jeans pockets and threw keys, cash, and phone on my desk. There was a text I must have missed during the movie. Or something else. It was from Becca.

I'm dying, was all it said.

CHAPTER

17

I CHECKED THE TIME Becca's message was sent: 9:14. It was currently 12:17. If I texted her back, would I awaken her from a pain-free slumber? What if she were back in the hospital? I had to try.

Are U OK? Are U dead?

After I sent the text, I turned on my computer and logged onto Skype. Chances were slim that Aunt Judy was still up and waiting for a midnight chat unless she had some seedy secret life I didn't know about. Maybe I would like her better if that were true. Like a Mullets Anonymous group or something.

Hello? Come in, Becca. Do you read me, Becca? I typed.

Nothing from either phone or computer.

To calm my nerves I played a video of *Troll* I downloaded last week. It was such a crappy movie, but the guy who played Atreyu from *The NeverEnding Story* was in it. And a weird plant lady.

I wished I could talk to Becca about what happened with Leo. It was exactly the kind of story my sex-obsessed bestie would have been dying to hear every drippy detail of. But instead she was just dying. For a second, I almost felt angry at her, which made me feel like the biggest dick in the world. How could I possibly be mad at my best friend when she was sick—possibly dying—with cancer just because I couldn't talk to her about Leo Dietz going down on me? Shame on me for even allowing a guy down there when Becca was so sick. Is that how she felt when she was doing *I don't even want to think about it* with Davis? Was this payback in the most disgusting form possible? I wanted to ask God, to talk to him one-on-one, but I couldn't decide if I even believed in him at the moment. Plus, kind of a weird topic. Death and sickness and sex and so much guilt—where did God fit into that?

As my internal moral battle raged, my Skype rang. It was not Aunt Judy and her mullet club but Becca. I scrambled to my desk chair and answered. The view of Becca was a close-up of her bald head resting on a stack of pillows in her bed. She looked tired and pasty. Her lips were dry and cracked. I wanted to pass her some lip balm through the computer, or a glass of water, or something to help. Once again, I could do nothing.

"Hey, Cueball," I joked. She laughed dryly but didn't say more. "How are you feeling?" I asked, wanting to know but not sure if she wanted to talk about it or pretend things were normal. I felt that way a lot about my dad.

"Like a bag of ass," she croaked.

"Whose ass? Because if it's mine, then you must be feeling pretty good." I was trying too hard.

"Can't laugh. Hurts." She held up a bandaged and bruised hand to her throat. "Tell me something good."

"Well, Leo went down on me in the backseat of my dad's car. And I met Bruce Campbell." Becca coughed, and I couldn't tell if it was because of what I told her or because she had to cough. The coughing continued. "Do you need me to get help?" I asked the screen. She shook her head no. A woman I didn't recognize appeared, her wide behind blocking the camera. When she was gone, Becca held a cup of water with two hands.

"Who was that?" I asked.

"Night nurse. Helen."

"Was she in the room when I just told you about the car scenario?" Becca nodded. "Is she still in the room?" Becca nodded again.

"But do go on," she eked out. I curled my lip in disgust, but Becca said, "It makes me happy to hear about it."

"I hope Helen isn't a prude," I told her, and launched into the story of the night.

When I finished, Becca told me, "Helen just crossed herself." I laughed. "I better go to sleep." And just like that she closed her eyes. I thought she might already be out.

"Are you really dying, Becca?" I asked.

She opened one eye. "The doctors say probably not, but it sure fucking feels like it." She closed her eyes again.

"Good night," I whispered at the computer. No answer. Becca was already asleep.

CHAPTER

18

I SLEPT IN on Saturday, spending most of the day in my room in case Becca called. I watched all three Basket Case movies, plus *The Toxic Avenger* and *A Nightmare on Elm Street 2*. While *Nightmare* wasn't as cheesy, weird, or gross as the other films, I always loved the premise of someone attacking you in your dreams. Plus, I heard Robert Englund, the guy who played Freddy, wore actual blades on his fingers and could cut an apple if he wanted.

The only Skype call I received was from Aunt Judy, who I ignored and didn't care about the consequences. I messaged a little back and forth with Damien and Brandon, and they invited me to a show that night, but I declined. I didn't want to have to talk about Becca or Leo or myself. There was no point in leaving the house.

Instead, my mom, brothers, and I shared a pizza and watched *Poltergeist* on TV. For a horror movie, it's surprisingly scary. Maybe I watched too many and was desensitized, but it seemed to me most horror movies were funny and gory but not necessarily scary. But

Poltergeist . . . the clown doll? I had second thoughts about leaving my Chuckie doll out after that. CJ hid behind the couch whimpering most of the movie.

I texted Becca at bedtime with a quick note.

Still Ok?

Ten minutes later she wrote back.

Can't stop barfing.

And that was it.

Sunday I worked all day, which meant hungover college students and tons of business. There was some game on TV in a corner of the restaurant, but we in the kitchen didn't give a shit and drowned out the jocular din with a musical din of our own. I anticipated the possibility of Leo coming in for a sub, and I wasn't sure how I felt about it. If he did, would we have to talk? Make out in the disgusting bathroom? I grooved on the rhythmic construction of the subs, and I didn't want that to be interrupted. When it turned out I wasn't interrupted all day by a visit from Leo, I was a tad disappointed. I wish I could make up my mind.

Before I left work, I texted Becca.

Do u want me to bring u a sub?

It was a long shot, with her puking issue. I was afraid she might say yes, which made me feel horrid. But I was scared to see her in person, not just in the grainy, poorly lit world of my computer screen. She texted back.

Too pukey. Too medicated. Thanx.

I kicked myself for my fear. How scary it must have been for Becca. I'm glad she didn't know what I was thinking. I had to hold it together for her, do whatever I could. I pulled out the Fuck-It List from my pocket. It was always there, transferred each time I changed my jeans. Nothing on the list caught my eye. It was either sex or food, and I wasn't in the mood for either. The guilt piled on me even more. I couldn't even do a simple task like number 2: Stick my tongue to a frozen pole, or one like number 18: Have sex with a football stud, and dump him the next day. "Jesus, Becca," I said to the list. "Just fucking get better, so you can do this ridiculous shit yourself." Then I berated myself again for my selfishness. The cycle was endless.

That night I did my homework in bed as *Troll 2* played in the background. Nothing like the original, it was so bad there was even a documentary made about how bad the sequel was.

My Skype rang: Becca in bed. I wondered if she had moved at all since the last time we spoke.

She greeted me with "Where's my sub?"

"I thought you didn't want it," I said, defensive.

"I'm kidding. Why are you so wound up?" Becca sounded better than the last time we talked. "I think I'm going to try and come to school tomorrow," she informed me.

"Why?" I asked, but I thought I knew part of the answer. Who wants to sit around feeling like shit when you can do something to make yourself forget?

"I want to get out of this death house. Plus, they're auditioning for the fall play."

"Becca, are you seriously going to try out? What if you can't—"

"I'm not an idiot. I'm just going to watch." She looked angry. I didn't know what to say.

"Do you have any other sordid Leo tales to tell me? Helen's not in the room."

I smiled. "Sorry, no. Just me and my hand. And I'm not telling you about that."

"Speaking of hands, Caleb has huge ones."

"Caleb? Homeschool boy?" I confirmed.

"I had Helen roll my bed near the window, so I could watch him mow the lawn. He looks a lot like Chris Hemsworth, I think. Sans the Thor lady hair."

"Maybe you can do a number eleven on yourself then."

"I'm being watched too closely to play with myself. Speak of the devil. Helen just walked in with my med cocktail. Gotta go."

"So I'll see you tomorrow?" I asked.

"Hopefully." She signed off.

I hadn't thought of Becca back at school so soon. Would the school year veer into semi-standard territory? It was hard to remember a time when life felt anything but abnormal.

I spent the following morning at school looking over my shoulder for Becca. I saw Leo once, and he gave me a smileless wave, not unfriendly but on his way to somewhere. He caught me on my way to lunch. "You feel like . . . hanging out?" At that point, it was unclear if "hanging out" meant just hanging out or taking each other's clothes off while surrounded by books.

"I can't today. Becca said she might come to school, so I want to stay visible." I guess I answered my own question as to where we'd end up.

"Is Becca well enough to come to school?" Leo asked, concerned.

"I have no idea. She seems to think so."

"Oh." Leo remembered something and dug into his front pocket. "Here." He handed me a key, similar to the one he used to open the book closet door. "I got you one." I turned the key over in my hand, wondering what exactly it meant. My face must have revealed something because Leo said, "Damn, it's not an engagement ring. I just thought maybe you'd like a key in case you wanted to go in there when I'm not around. No need to get all disturbed."

"I'm not disturbed."

"You kind of are," Leo pushed.

"Don't you have a class to go to?"

"Not really. But I'll find one to get away from you." He was messing with me, but he still walked away.

"Thanks for the key," I called after him.

"Sure," he called back.

Becca arrived while I sat at the lunch table with Damien, Eliza, and Brandon. She had on a striped winter hat, covering up her bald head. She walked slowly toward the table, and already I thought she looked thinner. Maybe it was her coloring. As she walked, a myriad of people came up to her to chat. I watched with a protective glare. Who were they to talk to my best friend before I did? I stood up and pushed past several of her fans. I grabbed her arm, then let my grip go soft when I realized how frail she seemed. We walked together to the lunch table, and Becca said, "I feel like a celebrity. Now I know I have to get famous someday." It was nice to hear her talk about the future as if she'd be alive.

Damien, Eliza, and Brandon bombarded Becca with hugs and questions, and I let her soak in the attention. At least it was people I liked and knew, not just cancer groupies.

At the end of lunch, Becca asked if I would walk her to the drama room so she could talk to Ms. Richards. She held my arm and waved with her free hand to her adoring audience. I almost punched Jenna in the face when she stopped us to squeal at Becca's presence. I pushed to keep moving, and Jenna faded into the hallway crowd. Before we managed to make it to the drama room, Becca's legs gave out. I held her up as best as I could, but my size wasn't helping me. In an instant, I felt her weight lift off me, and there Leo was holding up her other side.

"Are you okay?" I asked. I felt like I was always asking that.

"Can you take me to the nurse? I need to lie down for a minute." She sounded panicked. Then she puked, not a ton, but a dribble down the front of her shirt. I waited for Leo to make a grossed-out comment, but he just carried her along as though nothing happened.

"Sorry." Becca coughed.

As we walked through the halls, the same people who fawned over Becca minutes ago were now gawking at her like she had a disease. Which she did, although nothing they could catch. In fact, the crowd of people and their hordes of germs were much more dangerous to Becca than she could ever be to them.

When we got to the nurse's office, Leo carried Becca over to a plastic bed. The nurse called Becca's mom, and I pulled some tissues from a box and helped Becca clean off her face and chin.

"Thank you," she said. "My hero. And this is Leo?" So Becca—even when she's wiping puke from her chin, she's thinking about me and a guy.

"Yeah. Becca, Leo. Leo, Becca," I introduced them.

"Nice to meet you," Leo said formally. "I'll let you two have a moment." He backed out of the nurse's office.

"Well, that sucked," Becca said when Leo was gone.

"It wasn't that bad. You could have projectile-vomited."

"All over Jenna's face," Becca said dreamily.

"So it could've been better is what you're saying."

The nurse came back into the room. "Becca, your mom will be here shortly. Can I get you anything?"

"No thank you." Becca spoke with a sickeningly sweet baby voice reserved for doted-on patients.

"Do you need a pass, Alex?" Mrs. Kafcas knew me well from the era during freshman year when I had strep three times. She was nice and helpful and generous with the passes.

"Sure," I answered.

She ripped a pass off her pad and scribbled her signature. "You fill out the time when Becca's mom arrives."

Becca closed her eyes, and her breathing became even.

"Why don't you let her get some rest?" Mrs. Kafcas whispered. I could've sat there with sleeping Becca until her mom came, but that meant talking to her mom again. I wasn't up for the sad parent. I walked out and closed the door to the nurse's office quietly. Leaning against the wall nearby was Leo.

"She going to be okay?" he asked. I shrugged.

"Can we go somewhere?" I pressed, and he knew exactly where I meant.

When we arrived in the book closet, Leo sat down on a desk. "Do you want to talk about it?"

"That's the exact opposite of what I want. I just want to feel good." I looked at Leo. He walked over to me, put his hands around my back, and made sure of just that.

CHAPTER

19

BECCA AND I SKYPED the minute I got home from school. She sat engulfed in her pillow mound looking far less green than when I last saw her. "So that was—" she started.

"Putrescent," I finished.

"Thank you for sugarcoating things."

"You know you can count on me for that," I joked. "How are you feeling?"

"I wish you didn't have to keep asking me that."

"Sorry. But you did throw up, and my gallant guy-dude-friend-thing did have to help carry you through the halls."

"You still won't call him your boyfriend? What's that about? And did he think I was gross?"

"He didn't mention your grossness, at least not to me."

"Again, I feel so much better. And what about the boyfriend factor?" she prodded. While her words were on the normal side, her face looked pained.

"Who has time for a boyfriend? All that pathetic sexting and going on dates and meeting parents and proms and shit. I'm too busy taking care of you. Speaking of, is Helga in the room with you?"

"Helen. And, no, her knitting needles were driving me crazy."

"Careful what you say. Knitting needles make for excellent murder weapons."

"Always looking on the bright side, you are. Oh! Speaking of bright sides, I saw Caleb as I was coming home from school today."

"Was he naked?" I asked.

"I'll ask the pervy questions around here," she noted. Why wasn't she using more ChapStick?

"So was he?"

"I wish. He was taking out the garbage. Our eyes met as my mom pulled into the driveway. He smiled."

"Did you?"

"Barely. I was afraid I still had puke chunks in my teeth."

"That is quite possibly the grossest thing I've ever heard."

"From you, I'll take that as a compliment."

"I thought that was obvious. So when do you flash him next?"

"Try never. I look so gross now. Holes in my arms and on my chest, no hair. Did I tell you my eyelashes are starting to fall out?"

I shook my head. "Maybe we can write Caleb an anonymous note, and he can flash you back. We could add it to the Fuck-It List."

"How's that going, by the way?" Becca tried to adjust her position on the bed, and every movement looked strained.

I tried to remain composed. "Okay. I haven't done anything monumental. I'm saving some things for us to do together. Like the sleep on a beach one."

"That's meant to be romantic, Alex."

"Then how do you expect me to do it?"

"How about hop a train like a hobo?"

"Admittedly, that's one of my favorites. But, alas, no. Am I failing you?"

"Not at all! You did way more on it than I ever did, and it's my list." Becca started coughing but managed to calm herself before Helen arrived. "What about the last number on the list? Have you done that yet? I know it hasn't been that long, but I thought maybe you and Leo . . ."

I pulled the list from my pocket and reread number 23: Have sex with someone I'm in love with and who's in love with me.

"No. We haven't had sex yet. And we're not in love."

"Yet," Becca added.

"I'll let you believe that because you have cancer."

"You could totally love him, Alex. He's completely your type: big, weird, a criminal."

"He's not a criminal."

"Whatever. Fall in love with him soon, please, and have sex so you can tell me all about it." She yawned.

"Maybe I'll just fall in love with Caleb instead so you can watch us have sex from your window. That way I won't accidentally leave out any details."

"You better not. He's *my* homeschool boy."

"You've already branded him with your boobs. There's nothing I could do anyway."

We both laughed, and Becca's laugh turned into a cough again. Helen's big butt resurfaced. When the camera was free, Becca's newly scratchy voice said, "I have to go. Keep me posted on number twenty-three. I'm counting on you."

"And Caleb's counting on you. Sweet dreams."

"If only." She hung up.

From downstairs, I heard the garage door close and my brothers' clumsy footsteps fill the house with life. I didn't want to be alone, a rarity, so I headed downstairs and spent two hours splayed across the couch watching AJ and CJ destroy zombies. It wasn't quite as good as a movie, but their aggressive banter helped me temporarily erase the vision of Becca puking that was on repeat in my head. I must have been pretty fucked up to watch horror movie after horror movie, not to mention my brothers ripping intestines out of realistic dead humans, and only be disturbed by a little puke. Forgetting about that day, and so many others, felt like a constant goal. I hoped there would come a day I would want to remember.

CHAPTER
20

TUESDAY AND WEDNESDAY were regular school days in the sense that I went to class, nobody threw up near me, and Leo and I didn't spend any time in the book closet. His creative writing teacher was annoyingly holding him accountable for whatever it was he was working on, so I ate with my lunch friends listening to them talk about stage crew and trying to win me back.

"We miss you, Alex. The catwalk isn't nearly as creepy without you," Brandon told me.

"Yeah, and you already own enough black to blend in," Eliza said.

"You're really selling it, but I have an actual job and actual, you know, stuff I have to do with my evenings."

"Watching *Dead Hags 7* isn't 'actual stuff,'" Brandon air-quoted.

"If only that were a real movie," I mused.

I spent both nights working at Cellar and cramming in homework when I wasn't filling bread with assorted meats and cheeses. I liked the busyness, the mechanical yet artful nature of building a sandwich and delivering it to a hungry person. Sometimes I felt like the patron saint of subs. There probably already was one, from what I've read about saints, which wasn't much. Except that there's one for practically everything. I could totally fill out a pair of black wings. Do saints have wings?

Near the end of my Wednesday shift, Doug called back to me in the kitchen. "Alex, you have a visitor! Clean the bathroom first."

"I'll get right on that, Sir Subs-a-lot." Nobody tells the Patron Saint of Subs what to do.

I wiped my hands on my grungy jeans and stepped out to find Leo waiting for me behind the counter.

"Hey," he smiled.

"Hey," I repeated, not matching him in enthusiasm. I didn't want to get razzed by the college crew.

I stayed behind the ledge where we placed the subs ready for consumption. Leo leaned on the counter with his elbows, bringing his face closer to mine. The low lighting emphasized the freckles that seemed mismatched with the rest of his tougher exterior.

"Did you want something to eat?" I asked.

"Nah. Already ate. Thanks, though. Just stopped by to say hi."

"Picking up your comics?"

"Yeah. New Buffy and Walking Dead are out."

"Buffy comics any good?" I asked. "I liked the show."

"They're really good. Most of the time. They had this totally weird plot where Angel and Buffy had sex in space. I didn't quite get it."

I nodded as though agreeing with something. I wasn't sure how to respond to Buffy space sex.

"I guess I'll let you get back to work," Leo said as he drummed a little tune on the counter.

"Thanks, I guess," I said. "See you tomorrow, maybe?" The question felt awkward, like what I was really saying was "Will you be sticking your hand down my pants in the book closet?" But curious minds wanted to know.

"I have to meet with my teacher every day this week for my independent study, so I won't be able to, you know, hang out." He had some unbuttoning on his mind, too.

"Okay." I shrugged. No big deal.

"What about Friday night?" he asked.

"What about it?" I couldn't remember if we had talked about something, and I forgot again.

"Do you want to hang out? Maybe watch a movie? You know I've never seen *Basket Case 2* or *3*."

"That's right!" The thought of schooling a horror fan on the blinding brilliance of Basket Case had me jazzed. "So much different from Basket Case the First."

"Basket Case the First? Is that really what it's called?"

"No. But it makes it sound fancy. As fancy as someone with a mutant twin brother that used to be attached to his side can sound."

He laughed and shook his head. "Want to come to my house? My parents are going to a play. We can watch on the massive screen my dad installed in the family room."

Massive screen didn't resonate nearly as much as his parents going to a play. Potential book closet times ten.

"Yeah, okay. Sounds fun." We both smiled this time. "Speaking of fun, I have to go pretend to clean the bathroom, so . . ."

"Maybe I'll see you in the halls. Definitely on Friday."

"Bye." I waved. The anticipation of Basket Case and a parent-free house made heat rise to my cheeks. Maybe we'd just watch the movies, like we did with *Army of Darkness*. But that was in a movie theater.

I punished my overactive imagination by actually cleaning the bathroom. I don't know how clean it got because I didn't technically touch anything, just sprayed all the surfaces with a disinfectant cleaner. The next person to use the toilet would get a wet awakening on her ass. Serves any freak right for not squatting above the pot in this place. I threw a new urinal cake in the men's room and grossed myself out at the name. What sick bastard would call something you piss on a "cake"? Then my brain went into horror mode, at some psychopath's birthday party where the birthday cake was a stack of frosted urinal cakes with a candle on top. As I left the men's room, I laughed at myself.

"Someone's got a boyfriend," Ila sang.

"I was thinking about urinal birthday cakes, if you must know," I scolded.

I didn't have a boyfriend. I had someone to watch horror movies with while my best friend was too sick with cancer. Who somehow got me hot and bothered enough to clean a bathroom. Not a boyfriend at all.

CHAPTER

21

BECCA AND I TEXTED on Thursday whenever I could get to my phone without it being confiscated.

Becca: **Are u sick?**

Me: **No**

Becca: **Can u come over after school?**

Me: **Fuck yeah**

I had only Skyped with Becca since she started her treatment, and the only time I saw her in person was for her vomitous half hour at school. She said as long as I didn't bring any germs into her house I could come over and watch *Battlestar Galactica* with her. This would be my fourth time watching the series, Becca's fourteenth. She was obsessed with the actor who played Lee "Apollo" Adama, the son of the Galactica's admiral and number 21 on her Fuck-It List: Touch Jamie Bamber's butt. That was one of my particular favorite numbers because of the sheer impossibility of it. I thought that's what a bucket list was supposed to be filled with: things one could only dream of doing. Lucky for me, I guess, Becca had a more attainable list that I could help her with. Except for number 21. And maybe the one about the hobo.

When I arrived at her house, Becca's mom answered the door. She hugged me like we hadn't seen each other in months. The same hug she gave me after my dad died. I was lucky she didn't gouge out my eye with the bedazzled Star of David she sported. The only reason I ever regretted being a Jew was the fact that I couldn't wear big crosses around my neck like Buffy. Mrs. Mason's jazzy Jewish star didn't have quite the same vampire-repelling tendencies. It sure was big though.

I quickly retreated to Becca's room. Becca was camped out in her bed; vases of voluminous flowers and crinkly balloons were everywhere. Wadded up balls of wrapping paper littered the floor, and boxes of shrink-wrapped DVDs were scattered over her bed.

"Holy shit. It's cancer Christmas," I declared.

"Even my dad sent something. Six missed birthdays, but the possibility of his kid dying and he gets sentimental. Not that this thing is very sentimental." Becca held out a blocky stuffed animal hamster. "Watch this," she said, and squeezed its hand. "You're a toolbox douchecake," she spoke at the beast. It repeated back her words five times the speed, high pitched and eerie. The worst part was the way its tiny mouth moved, as though it was really calling me a douchecake.

"This is the first time I have ever liked your dad," I told her.

"You can have it." She tossed it to me, but the throw was short.

"I have a younger brother to terrify with this, thank you."

"Anytime. What do you think your dad would have gotten me?" Becca asked. The question froze me, repeated back in the chitter of the Chatimal.

"I don't know. I mean, I never thought about it. Do you?"

Becca looked exhausted, and her initial excitement at my visit faded from her voice. "I think about how he would probably say funny things. Maybe he'd come visit me in the hospital. Buy me a viper stuffed toy instead of a talking rodent."

It wouldn't have felt as bad if the dead dad we were talking about weren't mine. I was jealous. That my dead dad would bring things to my sick friend in her imagination. The subject needed changing immediately before I said the wrong thing. "What right do you have to get gifts from my dead dad?" came to mind.

"Somebody bought you Kim Kardashian's perfume?" I noticed a bottle on her desk.

"That's the ass of my dreams," she sighed.

"To look at or to have?" I asked.

"Maybe just to look at. Or, like, squeeze just once."

"You think if you squeeze Kim Kardashian's ass, her perfume comes out?" Laughs turned to coughs, and I regretted the hilarity.

"Come sit down and share in my spoils." Becca patted the blanket when she finished her coughing jag. I sat down next to her and looked toward the TV.

"Where are you?" I asked, regarding which season of *Battlestar* she was on.

"'Unfinished Business.' I just love that Lee and Kara finally have sex."

"Of course you do," I said. "This is a good episode. I love watching Starbuck kick Hot Dog's ass."

"That is good."

"If you were a pilot, what would your call sign be?" I asked. We'd had the conversation a million times, but it was one of our favorites. *Battlestar Galactica* pilots had really cool nicknames, like Athena, or truly dorky ones, like Narcho. "I've got one for you: Vixen."

"Ooh. That's a new one. But it's too much like Blitzen. I don't want to sound like a reindeer."

"What do reindeer sound like?" I joked. Becca nudged me softly. The top of her hand was poked and bruised. I willed myself not to gag. Real-life gore was so much more gory than the fake stuff. "Okay. How about Kumquat?"

"That's horrible!" she squealed.

"No worse than Hot Dog. What about me?"

"Yours would be Blackie."

"What?" I demanded. "That sounds kind of racist."

"I meant because you wear black. Like the color of your heart. Geez. I'll think of another one. How about Sleazy? Like the Ke$ha song."

"You and your Ke$ha." I had an epiphany. "You should totally make that your Make-A-Wish. Meeting Ke$ha."

"That's really good. But what about Jamie Bamber?" she mused.

"True. There's no way he could say no to you touching his ass if that was your Make-A-Wish wish," I claimed.

"So I should tell them my wish is to touch Jamie Bamber's ass?" she asked.

"I wonder if people ever make wishes like that. You know there's some twelve-year-old girl with cancer asking to flip tongues with Justin Bieber."

"You're sick."

"No, you're sick. I'm just trying to make your wishes come true."

A light tap sounded from Becca's bedroom window.

"What was that?" she asked. The same sound, louder next time, pinged off the glass. "Go see."

I slid off the bed and walked over to the window. Caleb stood in his bedroom with his window open, holding an envelope in his hand and waving. I slid open Becca's window.

"Hi?" I questioned.

"You're not Rebecca. Is she there?" Caleb's voice was powerfully low, his muscles so large it looked like his church retreat t-shirt could barely contain them.

"I'm Alex." I looked back at the bed to see Becca waving her hands no at me. "Becca is . . . indisposed at the moment. Can I be of service to you?"

"I have something for Rebecca. Becca? If you wouldn't mind giving it to her."

I fumbled with the screen until it rose up, and Caleb and I leaned out our windows toward each other. His arms were long and muscularly veiny. I bet if I fell from the window, he would have easily reached down with one arm to catch me. I grabbed the white envelope and landed back on Becca's floor. "Make sure she gets it, okay?"

"Sure. I will."

"Thank you." He nodded and closed his screen, then his window. I did the same, then dove onto Becca's bed.

"Holy shit. I bet it's a marriage proposal. He wants you to run away with him to an Amish village or something."

"He's not Amish, or he wouldn't be my next-door neighbor," Becca reminded me. "Open it. Last time I opened a letter I got a paper cut, and it's taking forever to heal."

I gingerly ripped open the plain envelope. On the front was written, "Rebecca."

"I like how he called you Rebecca. So formal. I'm telling you, he's going to ask for your hand in marriage. Wait, there would need to be some courting first."

"The last time his mom talked to my mom was probably fifteen years ago when she insisted on calling me that. They're not the friendliest neighbors to have, and my mom is too uptight."

"All this makes the proposal so much more romantic."

"Oh my god stop. Give me the letter."

Together we read it in silence.

Dear Rebecca,

I know you don't know me, but I have seen you coming and going from your house lately in less than your usual shape. I wanted to check in and ask if you are okay and if you need anything. As you know, I'm right next door and almost always home. Just throw something at my window.

Sincerely,
Caleb

P.S. I want to thank you for your visit to my window a few weeks ago. I hope that wasn't a lone incident.

"Ha!" I blurted. "He totally wants to see your boobs again! 'Lone incident.' I bet he had a lone incident after that, if you know what I'm saying."

"So sweet. Could he be any sweeter? I have to write him back."
A tinge of pink returned to Becca's cheeks.

We drafted a note to Caleb on some notebook paper. "Why don't you use your Hello Kitty stationery?" I asked.

"Please. I want to exude an air of sophistication."

"Becca, you stripped for him in front of his window."

"In a sophisticated manner."

Becca thought it best to keep the note short and sweet.

Dear Caleb,

Thank you so much for your thoughtful note. I am home now with cancer, Hodgkin's lymphoma to be exact. Maybe one day when I'm feeling better we can get a cup of coffee. I would be interested in hearing what homeschooling is like. I'm still hoping to finish up my senior year, so I can go to college. Will you go to college? I better go and rest now.

Fondly,
Becca

P.S. I would be glad to also give you a repeat performance when I'm better.

"I love how it goes from 'fondly' to 'I'll show you my tits again someday.' Promise!"

"Shut up and deliver the note, please."

"Do you have any wax you want me to seal it with? A spritz of Kardashian butt spray? A handkerchief?"

"Speedy delivery, Alex!"

I opened up the window and screen.

"What can I throw to get his attention?" I asked.

"How about a jelly bean? Someone sent me a fifty-flavor box." I picked out a black Jelly Belly, the dreaded licorice flavor, and threw it at Caleb's window. Within seconds, he appeared again. His shirt and face were moist with sweat, like he had been exercising. From the look of his body, I'm guessing he did that a lot.

I held up the folded paper, and he threw open his window and screen. We made the pass, he thanked me, and we closed up shop again.

I sat back on the bed. "Can I have some jelly beans?" I asked.

"Go for it. I puked a rainbow yesterday."

"They should put that in an ad."

We watched two episodes of *Battlestar Galactica* when Becca's mom called through the door, "Alex, you should get going. Becca needs her rest."

"PT scan tomorrow," Becca told me as I shoved my shoes back on.

"Is that going to suck?" I asked.

"I hope not." She shuddered.

"Me, too."

"Since it probably will suck, you have to promise to do something from the Fuck-It List tomorrow and email me about it."

"I'll try." I hiked on my backpack.

"You are not allowed to try; you are only allowed to do."

"This cancer is making you sound like a Jedi."

"If I were a Jedi, I wouldn't have cancer," Becca pouted.

"President Roslin had cancer." I pointed at *Battlestar Galactica* on the TV. "And she's pretty kick-ass."

"Great. All I need is some chamalla extract and Cylon blood, and I'll be cured." Becca oozed sarcasm. That was my job.

"Shit, Becca, what do you want me to say? I don't know what to do."

I stood with my backpack weighing me down as Becca and I said nothing. Finally, she broke the silence. "Sorry. I guess cancer has turned me into a bitch."

"At least you have an excuse." I smiled. "Let me know what happens tomorrow. Try to focus on your upcoming nuptials."

"I will." She broke a smile.

We said good-bye, and I left Becca's house, the guilt of the healthy friend weighing more heavily on my shoulders than the backpack.

CHAPTER

SCHOOL FELT LIKE an impediment to actual life. Tests, home-work, fucking gym class. Did any of it really matter? I spent much of the day staring at Becca's list. What if I died tomorrow? Would my life have been fulfilling? Would I have regrets? Would any of my thoughts or feelings matter once I died? Therefore, did anything that I did now matter?

I ran into Leo at my lunch hour, and he asked if I was still com-ing over that night. I told him yes, and as we parted ways I wondered why I didn't feel more excited. I liked Leo a lot, but something about turning a fantasy into a real person took away the excitement, the sexy mystery. At the same time, Leo managed to surpass many of my fantasies with an even more satisfying reality. Is that all that mattered anymore? Satisfaction? Immediacy? One moment of pleasure to eclipse the mundane, the horrific, the tragic? I didn't know what I wanted. Nothing felt important, not my current life, my future, my death.

Becca texted me near the end of the day.

Done w shit for a week. Maybe back at school next week. We can make out in the book closet.

Instantly my mood changed. I never knew what to expect from Becca's cancer treatment. It seemed like a lot of up and down, sick and normal, Regular Becca and Cancer Becca. If she were to be at school next week, it would mean jokes in the hall and instant updates on ridiculously unimportant things. Things that weren't worth typing into an email or holding for our Skype conversations. Toilet paper on shoes and whose hand grazed someone's ass in gym or who farted in AP Spanish. Laughter at lunch and looks in the hall that spoke louder than words. That's what I was missing from my life. Even alive, cancer took away my best friend.

AJ, Mom, and CJ were playing Jenga in the kitchen when I got home from school. "Whoa," I pronounced. "Am I in the right house?" I looked around suspiciously.

"We wanted to show Mom how expert we are," AJ explained.

"They've been playing at lunch in the school library," Mom bragged, the pride of her boys spending lunchtime in a library too great not to share.

"I remember that from middle school. Is Ms. Nelson still the librarian?" I asked, sitting at the table, careful not to knock it.

"Yeah. She's hilarious when we play Scattergories."

"Yes! We used to play that, too. And a lot of Guess Who for some reason." I missed that. The games. The innocence. Me and Becca in middle school.

CJ wiggled his finger into a precarious slot near the bottom of the Jenga tower and artfully slid out a block.

"Very nice move," I commended him.

"Thanks. You want to try?"

"Sure." I stood for better leverage and selected an easy target at the top of the tower. As I shimmied the block out of its hole, my hand twitched and the top half of the tower crumbled to the table.

"Jenga!" Mom yelled, with her hands thrown into the air. We all looked at her. "What? Aren't I supposed to yell that when it falls?"

AJ, CJ, and I looked at one another with eye-rolling glances and busted out laughing.

"I'm so glad I amuse you." My mom smirked. "So, pizza okay for dinner?" She stood and opened the menu drawer. AJ and CJ were all over it, but I had to decline.

"I have plans," was all I offered.

"Yes?" Mom goaded.

"I'm going to a friend's house to watch the Basket Case movies. He's never seen them."

"He?" Mom caught the slip instantly.

"Yes, Mom. There are boys who like horror movies, too. It's fascinating."

"I'm sure it is. Does this boy have a name?"

"Leo Dietz."

"So he has the same name as the boy you saw a movie with last week. Friday nights. Movies. If I weren't a confused old lady, I'd say it sounds like you're dating."

"It's called hooking up, Mom," CJ corrected her.

"You are both wrong, and promise me you'll never say those words again, CJ. Especially if it ever involves you."

"Then what is he?" Mom tried to hide a smile.

"I don't know. Why does it matter? We're not running away and getting married or anything."

"That's called eloping," CJ interjected.

"Have you been watching Lifetime or something?" I chided.

"He likes those movies where Tori Spelling gets stalked," AJ pointed out.

"Shut up." CJ punched AJ's chest.

"You shut up," AJ retaliated, and in an instant they were on the kitchen floor, on top of each other.

"Is that a scene reenactment?" I asked over their screaming.

Twin boy legs flailed, and a clatter of Jenga tiles rained down on top of them. "Enough!" my mom cried, and while she attempted to pry the gangly pair apart, I made my hasty exit, running upstairs to grab the Basket Case movies and calling "Good-bye!" as I escaped out the front door.

When I got to Leo's, his parents were in the front hall getting ready to leave. I was early, and I hadn't anticipated the dreaded meeting of the parents. I put on my most pleasant girl face, the one that says "I'm just a friend and your son will not be impregnating me this evening."

"So nice to meet you, Alex. Wish I could say we've heard a lot about you, but Leo doesn't talk to us much." Leo's mom was tall and polished, with his same dark, coppery hair. She wasn't overly friendly, and I wasn't sure if I actually liked her. Not that it mattered. Friends' parents were always at the bottom of the list of people I needed to like.

Or like me back. As long as it didn't get in the way of said friendship, neutral territory was fine.

Leo's dad didn't say anything, but he shook my hand when Leo introduced me. "This is Alex," was what Leo said. I was relieved he didn't precede it with "my girlfriend." They left soon after I arrived, and Leo and I did the awkward dance of *what now* in his front hall. I looked at the framed pictures his parents had along the wall. Gapped-tooth school pictures, family vacations on mountainsides, and military portraits of who I assumed was Leo's brother, Jason, covered the walls.

"He looks like you," I noted about Jason.

"Yeah. Except the halo over his head." Leo sounded peeved.

"What do you mean?" I asked.

"You know, every family has one kid who's perfect and one kid who's a fuckup. He's *not* the fuckup."

"I don't think every family has to be that way. Like, what about families with more than two kids?"

"They're lucky. The perfection and fucked-up-ness get distributed more evenly. Way less pressure."

I mulled over this theory and chalked it up to baggage I wasn't in the mood to delve into.

"I brought the movies." I held up the DVDs to change the subject.

Leo led me into the kitchen and opened the freezer. "What kind of pizza do you want?"

"Just cheese, if you have it."

As Leo cooked dinner, I moved into the family room. The house was very neat and looked designed, as though all of the knick-knacks were strategically placed instead of shoved onto available shelf space like at my house. I loaded the first movie into the player and sat down on a long, velvety gray couch. I kicked off my shoes and turned myself to lie down on the luxurious fabric. Leo entered the room, saw me, and took this as a cue to rest himself beside me. Instantly I felt my body heat up. This was my favorite position to be in with Leo: too close to read expressions, too tempted to have a conversation. We kissed and fumbled and groped and grabbed, but our clothes remained intact because, as I reminded him, "There's a pizza in the oven."

About ten minutes in, I pulled my face away from Leo. "You taste different," I said. "And smell different."

He talked into my neck. "I'm trying to quit smoking. Someone told me it tastes like a turd."

He quit smoking for me? That was a lot to put on a person. What would happen if we stopped whatever it was we were doing? Would he go back to smoking? Smoke more cigarettes just to spite me? Turn to crack?

The buzz of the oven put a pause on the couch session and my thoughts. So what if he quit smoking because of me? It was stupid to begin with, and he smelled a lot better without it. And if he started smoking again, not my problem. I didn't need another thing to feel guilty about.

Side by side we ate pizza, drank Coke, and watched *Basket Case 2*. Leo laughed at all the right parts, and I caught myself watching his face to see how he reacted to each scene. He was rather lovely. Nothing made someone more attractive than knowing they liked the same movies I did. It always disgusted me when people couldn't tolerate horror movies, or lumped them all into one dismissible genre, as though they weren't each their own work of art. Or piece of crap. But at least watch them and decide.

When *Basket Case 2* ended, I asked, "So what did you think?

Brilliant, right? The third one goes total crazytown. There's this part where Granny Ruth says, 'Oh Cedric, I see you've brought your lettuce.' It's hysterical—" Before I could continue, Leo was on top of me. He smelled so good, like laundry and pizza and gasoline, I couldn't help but pull his shirt over his head. Instantly my shirt was off, too. We attacked each other's clothing with mindless abandon. Instinctively I needed to be naked next to him, to feel nothing but his warm skin against my own. When all our clothes were off, we shivered together. Not from cold but anticipation.

We hadn't known each other very long, not in the talking-to-each-other-every-day sense. But I had watched him for years, followed his class schedules and smoke breaks, spied on him at horror movies and coffee shops. He felt familiar, safe. Leo had done nothing in his existence to make me feel bad, never touched me in a way that was all about him. I had never known a guy like that, and I had let them explore me, manipulate me, convince me that what I did with them would feel as good to me as it did to them. It never had. Leo helped me to lose myself. Not become someone different but transcend my life so none of the bad mattered. I wanted to be as close to him as I could. To feel what I had never felt with another person.

Our breathing was frenetic, like we couldn't get where we wanted to go fast enough. His hands were gentler than I wanted, and I grabbed one and wrapped it around my breast. I let out a sigh, and Leo reciprocated with a sound of his own. "Do you have a condom?" I asked. Life had been too cruel in the last year not to get me pregnant, or diseased if I wasn't careful. I couldn't trust my body to do the right thing, and I didn't want to have a conversation with Leo in the middle of this to talk past sexual partners. I didn't want to know. I just needed it to happen.

Leo rolled off me and stumbled upstairs. I quivered on the couch, every part of my body feeling tense and needing. Footsteps pounded down the stairs, and then Leo was on top of me again, ripping open the wrapper with his teeth. Quickly we were completely intertwined. Neither of us lasted very long. We couldn't have if we tried. Nothing I had ever done with myself compared to the grand finale with Leo. I shuddered, even after he collapsed on top of me. I willed the feeling not to end, and when it finally did I fell asleep almost instantly.

When I awoke, a knitted blanket covered my body. Leo, fully clothed, sat next to me on the couch eating Doritos and watching *Basket Case 3*. When he saw I was awake, he paused the movie. "I didn't think you'd mind if I started it since you've seen it a million times. Actually, I tried to ask you but you wouldn't wake up. Plus, you look really cute when you're asleep."

"I don't look cute." I sneered and tried to dress myself discreetly, but I felt Leo's eyes on me. It reminded me of Becca, of her flashing Caleb at her window the night before she started chemo. I dropped the blanket and dressed in full view. When I finished, Leo wore a huge grin. "Unpause," I said.

"Come here," he commanded.

I hesitated, and a ding sounded from the kitchen.

"Cookies are ready." Leo bounded off the couch into the kitchen, his bare feet slapping against the floor. When he returned, he carried a plate of steaming chocolate-chip cookies.

My face must have objected.

"What?" he demanded. "They're just the fridge kind. It's not like I broke a fucking egg. Don't eat them then." He looked put out.

Guilty as a bitch, I tried to hide my discomfort with his post-sex baking effort. "No. Cookies are good." Apparently, that was enough for him, and he squeezed up to me on the couch, barely giving me enough room to digest.

Ten minutes into *Basket Case 3*, I left to use the bathroom and when I returned found a nice, spacious seat on the opposite end of the couch. Leo seemed focused enough on the movie not to notice. When it ended, I collected my DVDs and told him, "Thank you for having me over." It sounded ridiculously formal after what we did, but I didn't want to get all sappy and relationshippy. The smell of fresh-baked cookies hovered around us.

Leo stood to walk me out, but I stopped him. "No, you stay on the couch. I can find my way out. Eat your cookies."

He looked at me quizzically but didn't make a move to rise again. "Thanks for coming," he said in a way that acknowledged the weirdness of the situation, the weirdness of me. "Hope we can do this again sometime."

I nodded, not knowing which part he was referring to.

"See you in school!" I waved overly enthusiastically and bolted out the door.

As I drove home, I berated myself for showing so much vulnerability during sex. It should have been no big deal. Except that it was a big deal. And sex with Leo was an even bigger deal. And the actual sex with Leo was most definitely the biggest deal of all. I mean . . . cookies.

Instead of doing something to make me forget the shit of my life, I had added something to make it a trillion times more complicated.

I knew then I had to end whatever it was I had with Leo.

CHAPTER

23

SATURDAY BECCA FELT somewhat better than she had been feeling, but not enough to leave the house. We spent the day together, camped in front of the TV, this time for a *Buffy* marathon.

"Maybe I should have my Make-A-Wish about Joss Whedon. Like, meet him or something."

"Screw that. You have cancer. Up the ante and wish for him to create a show about a badass bounty hunter and make you the star."

"Yes! Opposite Jamie Bamber!" she cooed.

"Speaking of muscular men, what's going on with you and homeschool boy?"

"I can't believe I didn't tell you. Yes, I can. I have total cancer brain—but he sent me flowers! Like, a bouquet he picked from his garden. With a note. It's over there."

I hopped off the blue chair and walked over to a wonky,

paint-dappled vase filled with wild-looking flowers, although not necessarily wildflowers. "Where's the note?" I asked, not finding it tucked into the bouquet.

"Oh. I hid it under my mattress. Mom and Helen are nosing around my room way too much. I think they suspect I'm smoking pot, which I'm totally not. I wish I were. It's supposed to work miracles on nausea. Maybe you can score me some!"

"Score you some? Who talks like that?"

"I do. Now get me some pot."

"Where am I going to get pot? You're the one who was all toking it up with Davis. Maybe you can call him in the army to score you some."

"What about Leo? Could he get me some pot?"

"Leo doesn't smoke pot. I don't think."

"That doesn't mean he can't get a quarter. Or a gram. However they measure it. Ask him. For me?"

"We'll see. Isn't it legal now for medicinal purposes? Can't you just get a prescription?"

"Can you really see my mom going to Walgreens to pick me up some joints?"

"Duly noted. Now where's that note?"

She accepted my weak commitment to getting her pot, and dug Caleb's note out from under her mattress. Inside a blue envelope was a neatly printed note.

Dear Becca,

I hope these flowers brighten your day just a little.
If you need anything, throw a rock at my window. I

might have something to help with the pain, too, if you're interested. Take care of yourself.

Wishing you well,

Caleb

"He totally wants to bone the cancer right out of you," I told Becca.

"You got *that* from the note? I thought it was much sweeter and homeschooly than that."

"What did he mean when he said he might have something to help you deal with the pain? Do you think he meant pot? Is he growing marijuana in his little homeschool garden?"

"There is no way. He's not like that."

"Ah, but Leo is."

"You know what I mean." I brushed off the insinuation that somehow Leo was pottier than Caleb. "But do you think that's what Caleb might have meant?"

"It's pot or his penis."

"I'd take either."

"Should we throw a rock through his window and find out?" I asked.

"I believe it was *at* his window. And no, not while my mom is home. I prefer this to remain a secret homeschool affair."

"That sounds pretty hot," I acknowledged.

"Speaking of hot," Becca transitioned, "tell me about your evening with Mr. Army Jacket."

I hadn't yet told Becca about my night with Leo. Parts of it felt too good to share with her, as though I'd be rubbing my ecstasy in her cancerous face. And other parts of it, where I looked like a dumping skag, seemed too stupid to burden her with when she was dealing with something so much bigger. Still, I knew how much Becca loved anything sordid, and it *was* a somewhat momentous occasion for me.

"Well, if you must know, I guess I kind of crossed something off my Fuck-It List. If I had one."

"Spill!" Becca's eyes were voyeuristically wide, which would have been creepy if we didn't already know every last perverse detail about each other's lives. That's what best friends were for, and we pushed that to the limit.

"So, yes. We had sex," I pronounced with a cheeky smile.

"I knew it! It's almost like I could psychically feel you doing it last night while I was in bed!"

"My god, Becca, contain yourself."

"Okay, not really, but I had a feeling."

"Could it be possible that having cancer has turned you into an even bigger perv?"

"Yes. It's a common side effect. Go on. How was it?"

That always seemed to be the question you heard after someone had sex. It was weird to me, like there was some sex scale that everyone was supposed to be measuring their experience by. People were so different in what they liked and knew and felt. Was that just the generically polite thing to ask after sex, like saying, "I'm so sorry for your loss" after someone died?

"I guess it was good. I mean, it was definitely good. Bordering on amazing?" I was at a loss for words. So much of what I experienced last night with Leo was purely tactile, not emotional or analytical. Was that how you knew when sex was good? Or was there more to it than that?

"So what part of it was on your list? Did you do something freaky?" She waggled what was left of her eyebrows.

"I am so renting you a male prostitute just to get you to shut up."

"Come on. Humor me. You've seen my list. What was it?"

"I had an orgasm," I declared. "With him."

"Ooh la la." Becca smiled, satisfied that she nudged the truth out of me.

"Yeah, but there's a problem."

"You're in love with him. I knew it! You know, you've proven that the endorphins released during an orgasm—"

"No, that's not it. I just feel like it's too much for me right now. Does it mean we have to start calling each other and sending cutesy texts? Go to stupid dances and exchange birthday presents and shit? I don't need that. I have my mom and my brothers to take care of and school and work and you . . ." I trailed off. I didn't want Becca to think I blamed her for anything, didn't need her to worry about me when she had to take care of herself.

Instead of worrying, though, Becca exploded. "What are you fucking talking about? Leo sounds like a great guy, and I don't just mean in bed. Don't put the blame on me just because you're scared to get close to him."

"First of all, how do you know that he's such a great guy? And second, I'm not scared of anything."

"He's a great guy because he's done nothing dickish since you started frisking each other. He carried me through the hall while I puked, for fuck's sake. And you are too scared of things. Do I have to remind you of Ronald McDonald?"

That fast-food clown scared the crap out of me with his red

mouth and huge feet. But he wasn't real. "Just because he hasn't done anything dickish doesn't mean he's a great guy."

"He is, though, isn't he?" She calmed a bit, watching me lose the argument.

"Yeah. He's nice. A lot nicer than I am." I chewed a cuticle.

"That's not too difficult an accomplishment, Alex." I smacked her leg. "Ow! Cancer leg!"

"Always with the cancer. And was that a cancer fart you just made?" I waved my hand in front of my face.

Becca rolled up in hysterics. "It's not my fault! It's the meds!"

We didn't mention Leo for the rest of the day, but that night I reviewed what was said and still came to the conclusion that I needed some space from him. Everything we did together just felt too good. Sooner or later, that would turn to shit as all good things did. I'd rather put an end to it myself than watch it unravel or blow up in my face.

After work the next day, I decided to fulfill a Fuck-It List entry— number 9: Bake cookies for the janitor.

I chose classic chocolate chip because the recipe was right on the bag. When it came time to mix in the chips, I lunged my hands into the batter instead of using a mixing spoon. The small chunks of chocolate and batter rolled in my palm with a massage-like effect. I could've stood there all day, until my brothers barged in and tried to finger their way into the bowl.

"Stop!" I yelled, and whacked at their hands. "These are for someone else!"

"Alex has a boyfriend," sang the twins.

"You guys are turds. I'm making them for the school janitor."

"Alex is dating the school janitor," AJ and CJ chimed in unison, as if they shared an idiot brain.

"Get out of here." I pushed them out of the kitchen.

They gave me an idea, though. Maybe I could soften the blow to Leo with some cookies. A sort of *let's be friends* peace offering. And these were real, homemade ones, not fresh from the fridge impostors. The janitor couldn't possibly eat all of the cookies anyway.

After the cookies finished baking and I doled out a few to appease my annoying brothers, I packaged them neatly into two Ziploc bags. One I labeled "To: Mr. Cooper, From: an appreciative student." I wavered over what to write on the second bag, how to address it, how to sign it. In the end, I simply wrote, "Leo."

He'd be fine. I'd be fine. We didn't even know each other that well—mostly in the biblical sense, as they say. (Were they really doing all that in the Bible?) I would keep myself busy with school and work and Becca, and he'd go back to whatever it was he did before me. He could start smoking again. I bet he wouldn't miss me at all.

CHAPTER

ARMED WITH TWO BAGS of cookies, I picked up Becca for school. On her head was a brilliant blue, bobbed wig.

"Attention much?" I asked as she got into the car.

"This may be my biggest moment in the spotlight," Becca declared.

"This will be one of many, Becca. Soon you'll star in a Hollywood blockbuster, date a movie star, burn out, land on a worst-dressed list, then have a miraculous comeback in some brilliant indie film, which will garner your first of many Oscars. I will be the only person you thank, of course."

"You have this all planned out, don't you?"

"Yes. And my career will go like this: Straight out of high school I write the next big horror franchise, totally revolutionary. I'll go on to a lucrative career in writing and directing, and I'll fall in love with Norman Reedus."

"Who's Norman Reedus?"

"You're kidding. You *must* have cancer brain to forget sexy hick Daryl from *The Walking Dead*."

"The one who always looks dirty?"

"They all always look dirty."

"The one with the crossbow?"

"That's him."

"Sounds like a plan."

"If we could only get high school to hurry itself up and get out of our way." Before we arrived at school, Becca had me park in a discreet spot on a side street. "You were right about Caleb having something for me." She dug through her bag.

"Please tell me he did not give you his detachable penis."

"Better," Becca said, and pulled out a joint.

"Homeschool pot, huh? Caleb's full of surprises. Maybe next he'll tell you he's really a demigod from Asgard."

"You want to try it?" Becca lit up the joint as if she had been smoking professionally.

"No. Unlike you, I have no excuse for acting like a glassy-eyed paranoid with the munchies in homeroom."

"Don't judge. It helps me eat."

"I'm not judging. Just promise me that when the cancer's over you won't turn into some Phish-loving pothead. I would have to divorce you."

"Duly noted," she coughed.

Becca walked with her hand on my shoulder into the school. I wasn't sure if she needed help balancing or the extra assurance on her big day back. I chose not to ask, pretending it was all normal. Before parting ways at my locker, I handed Becca the bag of cookies for Mr. Cooper. "You can be the messenger."

"But you made them."

"It's off your Fuck-It List, Becca. And, I might add, something you totally could have done yourself. If I weren't so trusting, I'd say you were taking advantage of me."

"I am, and you are one of the least trusting people I know."

Becca walked off slowly with the bag, and I watched as a concerned and adoring crowd swarmed her. "Let me know if you want me to call Norman Reedus and his crossbow!" I called after her. "And try not to scarf all the cookies!"

I waited to see Leo as the hallway crowd thinned, but he didn't show at my locker. That wasn't unusual, since we weren't really the locker-meeting types. Still, we did have sex Friday night and I did have a bag of cookies for him. Oh god, what if I didn't have time to explain that the bag of cookies was a consolation prize and instead he thought I baked him cookies *because* of the sex? I set the bag inside my locker and headed to first period.

Leo was nowhere to be found at lunch or art, our usual meeting times, but I was so busy fending off Becca's cancer groupies that I didn't mind. Breaking up with someone, even if we weren't technically together, was unpleasant for all involved. My guilt meter was pretty much ratcheted to full. Any more, and it might overflow.

The end of the day came, and still no Leo. I guess I'd postpone the cookie drop until tomorrow.

But tomorrow came and went, and still no Leo. I worked Wednesday and Thursday, and Leo didn't visit, nor did I see him in school.

I didn't want to call him or text him. First of all, he hadn't called or texted me in all this time, which wasn't very cool. But if I did, that just seemed like leading him on in some way. What if he was avoiding me? I was annoyed with the unknown, so I decided to do a little detective work.

Friday morning, Becca and I got to school early. I hadn't driven her since Monday, when the walking and talking and human contact seemed to knock her around more than she expected. Like a school-loving crazy person, she was determined to try again. I was glad to have her there to assist me in my Leo recon. She wore a red wig, shoulder length, with thick bangs. Apparently her mom went on a shopping spree at a costume shop and bought Becca no fewer than seventeen wigs. They didn't always help her feel well enough to stay in school all day, but at least she looked good. And gave her mom an excuse to go shopping.

We headed to the front office, and when Becca entered, it was like the moment where the birthday girl enters her surprise party. The secretaries screamed; the vice principal patted her back. My god. Cancer was a strange disease. I finally managed to get Mrs. Novak, the oldest and most crotchety of the secretaries, to recognize there was someone else in the office besides Becca.

"How can I help you, dearie?"

It may have sounded sweet, her calling me "dearie," but she only did so because she couldn't recall my name from the other fifteen hundred students, no matter how many tardies I got.

"I have a friend"—even that felt odd to say—"who's been absent this week, and I was wondering if you knew why."

"What's her name, dearie?"

"It's a he. Leo Dietz."

Mrs. Novak typed briskly onto her computer keyboard. The

juxtaposition of a prune of a woman and the shiny new technological equipment was always funny to watch. She mastered it a lot better than my parents could. Mom was always afraid that she was going to click some button that would make the computer implode. As if they actually built computers with a panic button.

Mrs. Novak's expression read that she found what she was looking for, and she looked up at me with sympathetic eyes. "I'm sorry, dear, but it looks like there's been a death in the family."

Those words caused a physical reaction so quickly in my gut that I had to hold on to the counter and rest my head. I flashed back to when our principal came to my English final to pull me out with the news that there had been a death in my family. I relived that moment all summer and every time I saw him in the halls wearing one of his tweed suits and Bears ties.

"Do you know who?" Becca came to my rescue, asking the question I couldn't.

"Sorry, dearie, it doesn't say in the computer. You can ask Principal Donovan—"

"No thank you," I interrupted her, and fled the office.

I found the nearest bench in the foyer, a modern, rectangular slab with no back, ensuring the least amount of comfort to discourage lollygagging and dillydallying. I sat down and cupped my head in my hands. Becca sat next to me and rubbed my back.

"See? This is what I'm talking about. If I hadn't gotten involved with Leo, then I wouldn't even have known about this and had to deal with it. You should not be rubbing my back." I ripped her hand off me.

"Alex, you can't seriously be mad that someone in Leo's family died."

"Why not? It's just another thing, Becca. Another layer of shit on the massive shit parfait that is life."

Becca snickered, and I shot her my death-ray look. "How am I not supposed to laugh when you're talking about a shit parfait?"

"How can you laugh right now? You have cancer! My dad is dead! Now Leo's dad could be dead. Or his mom. Or his brother."

"Alex, what am I supposed to do? Sit around crying all day? That's not how you deal with shit. You get to be all broody and mad and dark. Let me try to look on the bright side and laugh at parfaits." She snickered again, and I remembered the homeschool joint she lit up just ten minutes prior.

That got a smile out of me, but only a tiny one. "I have to call him."

"You don't have to. But unless your heart really is a lump of coal, you should."

"How about a text to start with?" I bargained.

"Sure," she mused. "I really want a granola bar."

I pulled out my phone and tried typing. All that came out were idiotic things like, "Who died?" and "I heard there was a death in your family. Sucks."

"Help me!" I pleaded to Becca. She grabbed my phone.

"How about, 'You haven't been in school. Hope everything is ok.'"

"But I know it's not okay."

"He doesn't know you know, and maybe he wants to be the one to tell you."

"Hit send before I chicken out."

"Done."

I waited until the last possible second to walk into first period.

No reply texts from Leo, but I couldn't bring my phone to class to keep checking. If a teacher heard the buzz of a text, that would be an instant confiscation until the end of the day. I placed my phone in my locker on top of the bag of cookies that was becoming less edible as the week wore on. Throughout the morning, I checked my phone in my locker every chance I got. Nothing. When lunch came around, I decided the wait was too much for me. But I wasn't ready to call Leo and sound like an asshole. Instead, I visited Mr. Esrum, Leo's creative writing sponsor. I looked through the glass window of his office door. Head down, he graded a stack of papers on his overflowing desk. I knocked on the door. He looked up over the top of his glasses and waved me in.

"May I help you?" he asked. He wasn't overly friendly, but I appreciated that in a person. Leo liked him, so I guess I did, too.

"Hi. I'm a friend of Leo Dietz . . ." I started.

"You must be Alex! He writes about you. I probably shouldn't have told you that, though." His sly smile indicated he was trying to make me feel good with this comment, but it had the opposite effect. I didn't respond to it.

"Do you know if Leo's okay? They told me in the office that one of his relatives died, but they couldn't say who. I thought you might know."

"Sweet of you to be so concerned." If he only knew how sweet I really was. "I'm afraid it was his brother, Jason. He was killed trying to dismantle a roadside bomb. Horrible." It *was* horrible. I wondered if Leo tried to picture the death, the explosion ripping his brother's body apart. I knew from experience that it didn't look anything like in our movies. "The funeral is next Wednesday. They have to wait until the body is shipped back." Mr. Esrum cringed, as though he knew he said too much. "I'm sure you could be excused if you wanted to go."

I hadn't thought that far ahead that there would be a funeral. That after I talked to Leo, there would be more.

"I'll think about it," I said somberly, and began backing out of the office. "Thank you," I mumbled.

"Alex?" He stopped me. "I'm sorry."

I closed his office door.

Inside I was seething. What was he sorry about? To me? I didn't know Leo's brother. I didn't know what to do at all, and he was sorry?

I ran down the hall to the only place I could think of and fumbled for my key ring to let me into the book closet. Once inside, I sat down at a desk and rested my head. The book closet felt so sad and empty without Leo. Old books that no one wanted to read, clocks telling time for no one but us, and there wouldn't even be an us again if I went through with it. My body wanted to cry, to release the pain and sadness that consumed it, but it wasn't *my* sadness. I wouldn't allow it.

I flipped through pages of Bradbury until I felt calmer, more focused. What would I have wanted from Leo if my brother died? I knew my answer was selfish. It was the same thing I had always wanted from Leo: to make me feel so good that I couldn't remember why I felt bad. But Leo was better than I was, and I knew it. I could tell by the way I caught him looking at me during movies. The way he laughed at things I said. I had used him because I needed him. Now he probably needed me. I didn't think I could be there for him, for what he needed from me. But I couldn't not talk to him. I remembered how horrible it felt when Davis, a guy I didn't even like that much, didn't call me. Just to say something. To acknowledge my pain.

The guilt had overflowed.

I left the book room, the hallways empty, and returned to my locker. Leo still hadn't texted me, but I couldn't use that as an excuse. The guilt punched me in my stomach until I couldn't stand it any longer. I had to say something to him, lest be devoured by my guilt. I found Leo's name in my phone and called. Every ring brought me further into panic mode. What would I say? Could I really help?

Leo's voicemail picked up. I nearly hung up, the dread of leaving a message overwhelming. But it was that or call again, and the weight of my conscience would have crushed me by then.

Beep.

"Hey, Leo, it's Alex. I heard what happened. To your brother. And I'm, um, really sorry. Shit. That was stupid. Never mind. I mean, let me know if you need anything. Bye." I hung up and threw my phone into my locker with a bang. The battery exploded out of its compartment. Instead of helping, I said the least helpful thing anyone could ever say to a person whose loved one died. I wished I could erase the message, suck the word "sorry" from the English language, and hack it to pieces with a rusty ax.

I ripped a cookie out of my locker and chomped on it, then spit it on the floor. It still tasted good. It should have tasted horrible, been filled with tiny, writhing maggots, and containing high levels of toxic sludge.

My guilty brain couldn't handle the rest of the school day, so I skipped out. Since the one thing that really made me forget everything—Leo—was also the reason for my pain, I opted for a gory movie brain fry. In bed with my laptop, I watched as topless girls received blades in their chests, as doppelgangers killed their good selves, as old ladies ate their grandchildren. It was sick and wrong, but it was all I could do. Once again, life had become too much to handle. The pile was too great. I pulled the covers over my head and listened to the screams.

CHAPTER

25

SATURDAY I WORKED all day, and the craziness of a nearby college football game kept Cellar busy. It would have sucked dealing with the morning tailgater drunks, but I was lucky to be making subs in the back. The day moved quickly, the Patron Saint of Subs doing what she did best.

I brought subs home for dinner, and my family ate together in the kitchen. AJ and CJ were still too young and clueless to have any plans for Saturday nights, and I needed to spend the evening with Becca before she headed for more chemo torture on Monday.

"I'll do the dishes," CJ declared when dinner was over, and proceeded to crumble our sub wrappers.

"You're such a help," Mom said sarcastically.

"So you'll raise my allowance?" CJ hinted.

"Only if you stop raising my blood pressure."

I heard my phone ring from my bag in the hallway, and I ran to get it. I assumed it was Becca asking me when I'd get to her house. But it was Leo. I forced myself to answer it.

"Hey," I said.

He cleared his throat. "Hey." Silence.

"How's it going?" Lame. Stupid. Dumbass.

"Pretty shitty. You?"

"Much less shitty, I'm guessing."

"Yeah."

"Yeah."

Was I supposed to be talking? When my dad died, people loved to regale me with their memories of him. It bugged the hell out of me. My dad was dead, and their personal stories seemed to belittle that fact, like, "He was your dad but I knew him first." I wish people were forced to write their stories of the dead down, so when the living were ready to hear those stories they'd be there waiting. The only story I had about Jason was from freshman year. He was a senior, and I had no idea where I was going for first period. But I really had to go to the bathroom, so I ducked into the nearest one assuming it was a girls'. It was not. One lone pee-er straddled a urinal. I gasped when I saw him, which caused Jason to turn around, still peeing. "The fuck?" he asked. I said nothing and ran out, lucky no one else saw.

That didn't feel like an appropriate story to share after someone's death.

"Could you come over?" Leo asked hesitantly.

I didn't know what to say. Becca was expecting me, and she'd be out of commission again soon. On the other hand, how could I say no when Leo's brother just died and he wanted me to come over? But on the other hand—or, I don't know, foot—my original plan was to break things off with him before his brother died. Now that death was involved, I only saw it as going one of two ways: I end it, or I become his intense, committed, *we can never leave each other because we've survived death together* girlfriend. I wasn't sure I could handle that. Still, I wasn't yet the world's biggest asshole, so I told Leo, "Sure. I can come now if you want."

"My parents are at my aunt's house." I didn't know if he told me because parents being home was always awkward, especially grieving ones, or if he was telling me "my parents *aren't home*." "So can you park on the street?" he finished.

"Oh. Yeah. Sure." It was a parking thing. "See you soon." We hung up, and I went upstairs to change clothes. Not that I needed to look nice, but I smelled like ham. Or maybe I wanted to look a little nice. Show respect. Instead of a printed t-shirt, I put on a plain, black t-shirt with my jeans and Chucks. Pretty much what I always wore, which didn't make it any less appropriately somber. I grabbed a few DVDs from my collection, just in case Leo, too, liked a little gore to keep his brain at bay. I also packed the cookies originally plated for a breakup. Now they'd look like a gesture for the grieving, which made me seem a lot nicer than I was. I called Becca to tell her of my change in plans.

"That's disturbingly sweet of you, Alex. Don't break his heart tonight, okay?"

"I'll try not to," I confessed.

"That's all I can ask."

"So what are you going to do now that your exciting plans fell through?"

"I had this idea of inviting Caleb over."

"Really? Is he allowed to leave his house after dark?"

"Good question. But even if he's not allowed, he could just sneak across our windows somehow."

"Sorry I'll be missing that."

"I'm not. I mean, I am, but not if I get Caleb in my room, if you know what I mean."

"You mean something sexy. That's what you always mean. Even if you end up playing Parcheesi, it'll be, like, strip Parcheesi."

"Brilliant! Now I have a plan."

"Details tomorrow, please. I promise not to ditch you again."

"You're not ditching me. You are performing a good deed."

"What? I can't hear you. The phone is breaking up." I crackled and fizzed into the phone.

"Be nice!" she yelled, and I hung up.

As instructed, I parked on the street in front of Leo's home. The house itself looked sad, the way the drapes hung, the newspapers piled on the driveway. I gathered the papers up and carried them to the door with me. Leo answered soon after I rang the bell.

I had never seen Leo with stubble. He seemed like one of those guys who didn't grow hair quickly, and there wasn't much on his face. Still, he looked older, worn. I stopped myself from touching his rusty shadow, not knowing if he wanted to be touched. He answered the question for me by wrapping his long arms around me and my backpack and holding on for what felt like minutes. I awkwardly clung to the random parts of his shirt I could reach in his tight grip. "I'm glad you're here," he whispered in my ear.

"Me, too," I said because I felt like I should. At a loss for anything to say, I told him, "I brought cookies."

He finally relinquished his grip and with a weary smile said, "Thanks. That's pretty thoughtful actually."

"You sound surprised." I had no right to be offended, but I played the part.

"No, it's sweet." He held my head in his hands and kissed my forehead, a painfully tender gesture.

"It's not. Really. I made them last weekend for the janitor for Becca's Fuck-It List," I blurted.

"Well, that part's sweet, I guess. So you brought me week-old janitor cookies?" He hadn't let go of my head yet, but leaned away to talk. We had never been this close except when we were *that* close.

"I brought DVDs, too. I didn't know what you'd feel like doing."

"Let's go to my room," he suggested, and took my hand. He led me upstairs, past even more family photos lining the walls. His parents obviously adored his brother, and the photos of Jason seemed to outnumber Leo three to one. Maybe it was just that Leo wasn't a part of anything, like Jason was. Fewer photographic opportunities.

Leo's bedroom was a mess. Not just a guy, throw-dirty-socks-on-the-floor mess, but scraps of paper, books, clothes, and even some car parts were everywhere. The single window was covered with taped-on cardboard.

"What happened?" I pointed at the window as I dropped my backpack on his bed.

"I guess I'm not so good at expressing my feelings," he said mockingly.

"Looks to me like you're quite good."

"My mom would have preferred a nice journal entry. Or if it were my brother, shooting a gun at an appropriate target."

"Do you want to talk? About your brother?" I said straight from the dead-relative handbook.

"No." He sat on his bed and pulled me down next to him. It was forceful but not painful. I could feel his need for closeness in the way he grasped my arm. I was glad he didn't want to talk because neither did I. If we talked, I might have said too much, told him about my dad just to make him feel better about his brother. Told him about Becca so we could both feel alive. But I thought that would change things between us. The more I said, the more we became something together, and I couldn't do that. So instead of talking, I kissed him. At first, his reciprocation was hesitant. I wondered if a cuddle was all he craved, that maybe sex wasn't the appropriate way for him to grieve. But soon he was on top of me, aggressively removing my clothes, sucking on my shoulder, squeezing my hips. I let him because I knew it could help, because I wanted the same thing. When we were together, inside and out, there was no death, no cancer, no past, no future. If his parents had been home, I cringed at the thought of what they'd have heard. We came together, so close we hardly moved. When we finished, we stayed wrapped around each other for five minutes. Ten minutes. I slept. I awakened. I slept some more. Only when my leg started tingling did I move. Leo snorted awake and repositioned himself to remain optimally close. I backed myself against him, and he encircled his arms around my stomach. I felt his breathing even again and assumed he was asleep. Then, in a faint voice, his mouth right up to my ear, he told me, "I love you, Alex."

I jerked upright immediately, as though hit with a jolt of electricity.

"I have to go," I said, already hunting for my clothes.

"What? No. Stay," he pleaded, but I moved fast and was soon tying my shoelaces. "What the hell, Alex?" Leo sat up, the blanket covering his lower half. "Because I said I loved you? I thought girls love that shit."

"You've known me, like, a month. And if you really loved me you'd know that I'm not a normal girl."

"Which is exactly why I feel that way about you."

"You're confused. You're grieving. You just had a massive orgasm. You didn't mean it."

"I've been thinking it awhile, Alex. Why is it such a big deal? I didn't expect you to say it back. I knew you wouldn't. But you don't have to be such a bitch about it."

"Fuck you. I'm a bitch because I don't want you to be in love with me? Well, then you're an asshole for being in love with a bitch." I stood up and slung on my backpack.

"You know what, Alex? You're a pussy. You put up this tough girl act, but you can't handle anything," he said through gritted teeth.

"I can't handle anything? I didn't break my fucking bedroom window, did I? I'm handling, Leo. A lot. My dad. Becca. Now you? How much more am I supposed to handle?" My voice cracked, my cue to leave. No way was I going to let Leo see me cry. I turned away from him and dug the cookies out of my backpack. "Here." I threw them onto his bed, not looking at where they landed, and stormed out of his room.

"Alex!" Leo yelled from his room. I didn't look back. He didn't follow. I didn't hesitate to start my car and drive away.

Becca had asked me to be nice. Instead, I was a monster.

CHAPTER

MONDAY CAME WITH NO contact from or with Leo. Becca implored that I call him on Sunday, but I had nothing to say. Everything I already said was asinine, and everything I'd say next would probably be worse. Becca started chemo again and was so exhausted and sick from the drugs, the only news I heard from her was a text that said, "Take my head. Please."

I wasn't sure if she was trying to be funny or completely delirious, and when I texted her back, "Where should I take it?" she didn't respond. I was done reading her mom's sugarcoated anecdotes about Becca in the hospital. The last one I read freaked me out big-time.

Becca is sicker than I had imagined, but I pray each morning and night that God will see her through. He spoke to me, told me to take care of myself, too, so yesterday I had a facial and manicure. . . .

Did Becca's mom actually believe God spoke to her? And what was he saying? *Go to a spa.* It all seemed so backward, talking to God for help, preening, when her daughter was wasting away in her single bed.

I had no interest discussing any of this with the stage-crew lunch table. They didn't know Becca's mom at all, and what I really couldn't stop thinking about was Leo. But seeing as I never told the lunch table about Leo, any talk about him would most certainly be followed by a diatribe from Brandon about the dangers of secret lovers. I could hear his voice proselytizing, "If you couldn't tell us about him, then there must be something wrong with him."

Problem was, there was nothing wrong with Leo. I just couldn't deal with him—or everything that came with him before and after the death of his brother—plus be there for Becca and my family.

That's what I kept telling myself.

I worked Tuesday after school and pretended it didn't bother me that Leo hadn't visited. Wednesday was Leo's brother's funeral. Mr. Esrum told me I could go, and as much as I didn't want to, I knew I had to. I stopped by Mr. Esrum's office before first period, and he gave me a pass to excuse me for the rest of the morning. My mom could've written a note or called in, if she knew what happened.

I didn't tell her.

Leo was merely a blip of a boy who was a friend on her radar, and I feared adding death to the equation would set her off. One of my brothers' friends' uncles died recently, and my mom spent the night locked in her room.

Mr. Esrum suggested creepily that we carpool, but the idea of sitting in a car with a teacher had Lifetime movie written all over it. I thanked him but declined.

I hated my outfit. It was dressier than what I usually wore, involving a long, black skirt, black tights, and black Mary Janes. But the only clean shirt I had to wear was a beat-up black t-shirt. I never went anywhere that required dressing up, and the only dress I owned that was suitable for a funeral was the one I wore to my dad's. There was no way in hell I was leaving the house in that.

I drove to the church Mr. Esrum so kindly Google-mapped for me. I had never actually been to a church. It wasn't like my non-Jew friends were asking me to hang out in pews on Sunday mornings. Lining the church driveway were people, possibly veterans, holding American flags. In the distance, I caught sight of an American flag–covered coffin being removed from a hearse, military men and women in their dress uniforms saluting.

I parked on the street and watched from my car. I hadn't expected so many people in uniform. I felt schlubby, inadequate, useless. When the family, black-suit-clad Leo included, followed the coffin into the church, I stayed in my car. When the rest of the funeral-goers were safely inside the building, I still didn't budge. Who was I to listen to people talk about Jason? I didn't know him, except for watching him pee. He literally said two words to me his whole life. I felt like an intruder, the little Jewish girl who busted the shit out of Jason's brother's heart, attempting some semblance of penance by barely playing dress-up and sitting in my car.

I thought about driving off. Going back to school, or somewhere else until my pass wore off. I tried to remember my dad's funeral, not so long ago but a painful blur of torment. Did I even notice who was there? Did I once look at the guest book to see who cared and who didn't?

Yes I did.

And the one glaring omission was Davis, my supposed-to-be boyfriend.

I wasn't supposed to be Leo's anything. But I didn't want to be his glaring omission either.

I waited in my car, deciding I could follow the family to the burial site. Being there would be enough. It had to be enough.

After about a half hour, sweat gathering underneath my skirted knees, people began to file out through the church doors. Another group loaded the flag-adorned coffin back into the hearse. Leo, head lowered, joined his parents in a black car. When other cars began to follow, I drove behind them.

We parked in an orderly fashion along the side of the cemetery road, uncomfortably narrow. People exited their cars onto the grass, high heels and polished shoes sinking into the dirt. I tried to blend, my height hiding me among the other mourners. There were more veterans with flags, more soldiers in dress uniforms, so young they barely looked older than me.

Leo and his family sat under a tent in front of the American coffin. They were tall, but I couldn't see much more than the backs of heads. A small group of soldiers, two of which were girls, *women*, held guns and shot them into the air. I had never been that close to real guns. The explosion of sound, then ringing of silence, shook me twenty-one times. Then a lone soldier played taps on a trumpet. I wondered how he got the job, if he was a trumpet player before he went into the military or if they have music school there where the only song they learned was taps. Did they know Jason? Was this their job in the military? Go around to funerals and perform death rituals? It seemed harder than going to war itself.

Together a group of soldiers folded the flag from the coffin. I was terrified for them, that they'd mess it up, there were so many precise steps. I thought about them studying that, too, that being part of the military wasn't just about going to war but dealing with what happens as a result. Was there any joy in it at all?

Would there ever be joy again?

I watched the back of Leo's family's heads. I remembered the feeling of being a family member sitting in the chairs, the special place that was the worst place to be. I wondered who watched me, wanted to see me cry. My mom had sat next to me, sobbing uncontrollably. It had been my job to hand her tissues. No one gave me the job, but I didn't want my mom to gross people out with the pool of snot under her nose. That's what I thought about: my mom's snot. Anything to get through. And there I was at someone else's funeral, hoping Leo didn't need a tissue.

As my brain spun with funerals past and present, the end of the service caught me off guard. I awkwardly tried to hide myself behind the Dietz giants and military uniforms. I went to the funeral. Was it necessary for me to be one of the sorry people? I couldn't do it. I couldn't do anything.

As the rest of the mourners milled about, held flags, shook hands, I tried my best to subtly make my way to my car—my head down, not risking the opportunity for a forced, sympathetic look. Not that I wasn't sympathetic, but a look wasn't what Leo or his family needed. I breathed out with relief when I got to my car door undetected. I made the mistake of looking up toward the funeral, and in that quick second my eyes led directly to Leo, who was looking right at me. We were far enough away that I didn't attempt mouthing anything to him, not that I had something to say. All I could offer was a slow nod of my head. Leo did the same. Then someone engulfed him, a blubbery hug, and I made my escape.

Maybe it was enough that I was there. Maybe he knew I cared even if I couldn't talk to him. Maybe it didn't matter at all.

I thought about skipping the rest of school that day, but I had a quiz in history that I didn't want to have to make up. Annoyingly I reached the school building at the same time as Mr. Esrum. He gave me a conspiratorial face, as though we'd just shared something momentous. But we hadn't shared it. Everyone was alone at a funeral. "Lovely service, wasn't it?" he asked. Funeral small talk was so gross. I shrugged. "Hopefully Leo will be feeling more up to it second semester."

"Up to what?" I asked.

"I'm sorry. I assumed he told you. Leo is taking the rest of the semester off to do homebound. It's very common for kids to need time off when there's a death in the family."

I knew that all too well. Even though I didn't.

"I'm sure you'll see him, though." Mr. Esrum was fucking clueless.

"I have to get to class," I told him, and walked as fast as I could to the book closet. I fumbled with the key and swore repeatedly until I managed to unlock the door. Once inside, I was lost. This tiny space and I was lost. I knocked at a stack of Shakespeare, and it spilled to the ground. That wasn't enough. I kicked another stack, and down it went. I slipped on books, which made me angrier, and I punched a shelf. Books rained down in every direction as I kicked, hit, shoved at any semblance of neatness and order. When nearly every book lay in a heap on the floor, I collapsed on top of them. Corners jabbed my ribs, my neck, my face, and I welcomed them. Then the tears came. I couldn't stop them. I imagined I was Alice through the looking glass, filling the floor with my giant tears, the absorbent books sopping them up until the pages floated along like soggy crackers and I floated away with them.

CHAPTER

27

WINTER

BECCA FINISHED HER LAST round of chemo yesterday. She claimed it was at maximum toxicity, and I didn't doubt it. It seemed like the chemo was meant to kill everything except her. Sometimes she could barely lift the remote, and other times her head hurt so badly all she could do was silently cry.

School and life had been lonely, but not much different than it had been over the summer. I worked, watched movies, helped my mom out. Talked to friends at school, but that was about it. Whenever Becca felt up to it, I went to her house. My mom had taken up making a different casserole for each visit. I don't think Becca managed to try even one. The smell of her bedroom had evolved. In eighth grade, Becca went through a fragrant phase after her aunt Vicki visited the Caribbean and bought her a perfume called White Witch. Becca thought this was the coolest thing ever, never mind the nose-piercing smell. She managed to collect dozens of bottles and sprayed everything she owned with the scent. Thankfully, she finally ed on to a new smell, one of Britney Spears's concoctions, but the White Witch bottles still remained in a box in her closet. The White Witch smell hung around too, and I couldn't be in her room without flashing back to innocent dances and early curfews.

Her room smelled nothing of White Witch anymore. The smell was a combination of disinfectant, Jell-O, and puke. I wondered if Becca could smell it. Or if her nose was immune to it, like how grandparents have an old-person smell that I'm sure they're not aware of.

Some days the smell in Becca's room was so bad I almost suggested pulling out the old vile of White Witch and coating the air with it.

I watched helplessly as she dealt with the side effects: constant nausea, puking, not being able to walk, not being able to see, not to mention the tubes and holes and weight loss and not wanting to eat. Why did this happen? To Becca, and to anyone? Why can someone get so sick that the only way to get better is to make them more sick? It's like the world's longest exorcism. It doesn't make sense that I can chat with someone live on a tiny screen, that governments spend billions of dollars on war and mayhem, that actors make millions of dollars to just look pretty and skinny, yet no one can fucking figure out how to cure cancer without torturing people.

The other day Becca's mom said, "Thank God" about something. It wasn't anything important enough to remember or anything big enough to warrant divine intervention, but she felt the need to thank God, something she'd been doing a lot of recently. Becca didn't hesitate to correct her mom, "I don't believe in God."

"What?" Her mom looked shocked, uncomfortable, as if saying

she didn't believe in God would somehow make Becca cursed. If she could be more cursed than she already was.

"I don't believe in God," she repeated.

"I suppose that's understandable, though I'm sure you don't mean it," Becca's mom conceded. "I'm going to believe in Him and keep praying for you."

"That is just wrong, Mom." Becca's mom had hit a nerve. "What kind of god do we have to beg to make us well? What kind of god allows people to get this sick? And not just get sick, but have months of pain and misery? Is it some kind of vengeance? A lesson He's trying to teach me?"

"God gives what you can handle."

"So it's a test? Let's see how much shit Becca can endure, so she can come out a better person on the other end? Was I that bad a person to begin with?"

"It's not just what *you* can handle, Becca. And God doesn't control everything, but He can help us get through."

I wondered if Becca's mom had always been this religious and I hadn't noticed, or if this was a direct correlation to watching her daughter disintegrate.

"I don't want to believe in a god who can help me because I can't believe in a god who would let something like this happen in the first place."

Becca's mom was shaken. Maybe she was holding on to the belief that God would save Becca. That if she prayed long enough and hard enough, she'd get better.

I didn't know what to believe anymore. Here I was, surrounded by death and sickness, guilty for the tiniest crumbs of pleasure

I allowed myself: ice cream, horror movies, and the selfishly selfish act of finding happiness in making Becca laugh. Where did God fall into any of that? I didn't want to think about it. I didn't want the blame, or the hope, to be on someone else. So I carried on, waiting for whatever was to come, with or without God's help.

CHAPTER

28

I HADN'T SEEN LEO since the funeral. I told myself he needed space, that he wouldn't have taken a semester off if he wanted to be around people. I tried to convince myself that somehow we were different; that my absence was appreciated instead of begrudged. But really, why would he want me around after the way I treated him? I went with that, but I thought about him all the time. When a movie came on TV that I thought he'd like, or I read about what celebrities were coming to Dead of Winter Con next month. I wanted to call, or at least text. Once I managed to force my fingers onto my phone.

Got a 2nd copy of Frankenhooker. You want?

Two painful days later, I heard back from him.

No

Like I said, ouch.

Becca tried to keep things light, when she could willingly move her body. We made a list of things to do at Dead of Winter Con, and we planned on going, no matter what state she was in. I told her if she couldn't walk, I'd push her around in a shopping cart.

"What if I throw up?" she asked.

"Who would know that was real and not just some realistically sick-ass costume?"

Just one day earlier, Becca got the news everyone was waiting for: chemo was officially over, at least until after radiation and the results came back.

Then why was she still so fucking sick? Instead of cancer being over, Becca was in total, all-consuming pain. Her joints ached, her head hurt, and the nausea was just as bad as it ever was. Whatever they used to kill the cancer was beating the shit out of her insides nonstop. Her meds made her groggy and incoherent, and she still seemed to be in so much pain.

The last time I visited, packing Mom's patented tuna noodle casserole, she slept most of the time, except when she woke up to whimper. I stayed out of obligation and guilt, not because I liked it. There was nothing I could do for her, and even being next to her didn't matter when she was unconscious. Her mom came into her room every few minutes, and each time she told me, "You're such a good friend, Alex." It made me feel worse. Especially the fifth time she added, "God bless you."

The only thing that lightened my mood was reading the love notes Caleb had been writing to Becca for the last couple months. He was a smart guy and an old-fashioned romantic.

My dearest Becca,

Today I chose to study the films of Lillian Gish. She reminds me of you, and I envisioned you on the screen someday as bright a star as there ever was. My sister is still in her baking unit, and she made some chocolate-chip cookies using coriander. I'll make sure to drop some off. I don't know if you can eat them now, so she froze some for when you can.

Looking forward to our next visit, Caleb

If a guy wrote me a letter like that, I'd be embarrassed to the point of burning the paper. But it suited Becca. She deserved to find some joy in the shitty quagmire of her life.

During the quietude of her bed rest, I tinkered with the idea of getting in touch with Leo again. It killed me that he ate away my brain like that. Maybe it was just the loneliness of being next to someone who couldn't even talk to me, who had stacks of love notes tucked under her mattress. But she deserved those love notes. I deserved the loneliness. It was self-imposed, after all.

CHAPTER

THE HOLIDAYS CAME AND WENT. They were the first without my dad, and therefore had more sadness and reflection than anticipation and celebration. Becca and I exchanged gifts aboard her bed. She gave me some hardbound classic *Tales from the Crypt* comics, and I bought her a *Battlestar Galactica* t-shirt reading, "I ♥ Fat Apollo." It was a hilarious misstep on the part of the show's creators, making the usually buff Apollo into a doughy mess to show the passage of time (other characters just got new hairdos). Even better was how quickly and effortlessly he got back into shape. And even better than that: A shirt was created to commemorate the gaffe.

It would be the perfect shirt for Becca to wear to Dead of Winter Con, where none other than Jamie Bamber, aka Lee "Apollo" Adama, would be appearing in the autographs area. That would finally give us a chance to get back to the Fuck-It List, which had fallen into obscurity soon after Leo's brother's death. Except for one item.

"I did it!" Becca announced over Skype one afternoon. She was having a good day and spent almost the entire time at school "playing a norm" as she liked to call it. By the time I came home from school, she was back in her pj's.

"Did what?" I assumed it had something to do with one of her video games, which she had become increasingly addicted to thanks to too many hours a day in bed.

"Number eleven on the list."

"Some of us don't have the list memorized," I reminded her.

"Here's a hint: It's one of the first ones you did. By yourself. Something I had never done *by myself.*"

"Ooooh. Number eleven." I recognized it now as the masturbating number. "Mazel tov," I congratulated her.

"It just felt like the right time. No one was home, and Caleb left a note by my door. I imagined him sneaking in my window."

I interrupted her, "Becca, the beauty of number eleven is that I don't need to know what you did or what you thought about. But I'm happy for you. See? Even cancer can't stop you from touching yourself."

"Fuck cancer!" she exclaimed.

"Fuck cancer!" I reiterated.

A few weeks later, Becca would have the chance to accomplish number 21: Touch Jamie Bamber's butt. I couldn't wait. Dead of Winter Con was a decent-sized horror/sci-fi convention filled with panels of B-grade (or lower) celebrities sharing their memories of working on mostly defunct TV shows and straight-to-DVD movies, with plenty of vendors selling their gory wares. Some years there was no one I'd pay money to see, but I still loved the atmosphere. People dressed up in homespun costumes, some based on movie characters, others pulled from their sick and twisted minds. My kind of people. This year I'd wear my usual clothes, since they were already zombie-based, and I'd add some blood and dangly bits to my arms and face to make it realistic. Becca planned on wearing her Fat Apollo t-shirt, in hopes of charming the pants off Jamie Bamber. Not literally, of course, although number 21 didn't specify whether or not his butt had to be naked.

I hadn't had something like this to look forward to in months. Not since the *Army of Darkness* showing with Leo.

Leo.

I wondered if he would go to Dead of Winter Con.

I wondered if I'd see him.

I wondered if he still loved me.

I tried to forget he said that. It seemed unreal, a spontaneous proclamation born from ejaculation and mourning. I told myself over and over that he didn't mean it. And then I berated myself for even thinking about it. For thinking about him. I'd catch myself, in the early morning times when I was only half awake, when I allowed myself to feel good, thinking of Leo. I remembered what it felt like to be together, how being with Leo felt better than being alone. I relived his touch with my touch, but it wasn't the same. I'd hate myself in the shower afterward. It was just easier to hate myself.

CHAPTER

30

THE WEEKS BEFORE Dead of Winter Con, Becca began feeling a little better. She was still tired, still in some pain, but her hair was sprouting the tiniest bit so nothing could get her down. She started radiation, a process not nearly as bad as chemo.

"I still feel like shit, though," Becca confided one afternoon from her bed while I sat in her blue chair. She wore a pair of pajamas covered in pictures of sushi, some of her cancer swag. Every time I saw her she was in a different pair of pajamas. She swore she had more pj's than regular clothes. "And check this out." Becca lifted her shirt to show me a pattern of black lines drawn on her chest.

"If you wanted a tattoo, I could've done something cooler than that," I told her.

"They drew them on me at the hospital so every time I have radiation I'm lined up in the exact same spot. It seems so unmedical, like there should be more to it than just pulling out a permanent marker and some waterproof tape to cover it."

"What would happen if they didn't align you correctly?" I asked, picking at a box of chocolates dropped off by her homeschool loverboy.

"They'd burn up my organs, I guess. In the olden days they'd actually tattoo the marks on your body."

"The olden days before Sharpie?"

"Yes. The Sharpieless days of yore."

It was fun hanging out with Becca like that, but everything was different. Just looking at her was a constant reminder of the past four months. Her hair, of course, but even when she lifted up her shirt I could see how thin she'd gotten. So many months of nausea killed her appetite, and the combination of the illness, drugs, and malnutrition zapped her energy. Nearly every time we watched a movie together, Becca fell asleep. I didn't know how she—how we—would make it through Dead of Winter Con. Becca's mom rented a wheelchair a month ago, but Becca refused to use it. It was funny to watch Becca's vanity randomly show its pretty little head. She didn't seem to mind the baldness and wig wearing, but when it came to her standing on her own two feet she was adamant. "I don't mind leaning on someone if I'm having trouble," she told me. "In fact, I have to admit I love the attention. One day at school, Edgar Abbott practically carried me out of French and down the hall."

"Who's Edgar Abbott?" I asked.

"He's on the football team. I think he may be a quarterback. Or a halfback."

"It's all jock to me," I said.

"He smelled surprisingly good," she mused.

"Don't let Caleb hear you," I warned her.

"Caleb could crush Edgar Abbott. Not that he would. Caleb's a pacifist. Next year he's thinking about joining the Peace Corps," Becca said wistfully. "I might join him."

"Say what? Is this your cancer brain talking?" I walked over to her and spoke loudly into her ear. "Becca, are you in there? This person says she wants to join the Peace Corps."

Becca shoved me with a frail hand. "I didn't say it was definite, but he got me thinking. The cancer got me thinking, too. If I live, maybe I should do something more important with my life than pretending to be someone else for buttloads of money."

"(A) You mean *when* you survive, and (B) there is nothing more important than starring in one of my horror masterpieces. It's on your Fuck-It List, remember? I didn't see anything about saving other people's lives."

"Your capacity for empathy never ceases to amaze me."

I knew Becca was joking, making fun of me for sounding callous. But part of me knew she was absolutely right. The one thing I rarely expressed was empathy.

Which brought me back to Leo.

"I was thinking of inviting Leo to Dead of Winter Con. Well, maybe not inviting him, but seeing if he was going."

"I think that would be a fine idea." Becca pursed her lips, holding in words she didn't think she could say.

"What?" I demanded.

"Nothing. I said I thought it was a fine idea, and I do. You should do it right now."

"Like, right now?" I asked as though it were Becca's decision.

"I'm not getting any younger."

"I can tell. You're starting to talk like an old broad."

"This old broad says you need to call him ASAP. My bunions are killing me."

"Would you settle for a text, Madame Bunions?"

"Only if I get to read it."

"I'll get your bifocals."

I stared at my phone for a minute before I concocted this brilliant work of art:

Hi. Are u going to Dead of Winter Con? If so, I'll see u there. This is Alex, btw.

I stupidly hit send before I showed it to Becca, and when she read it afterward she berated me for it.

"Really? You haven't talked with the guy in months—after you had sex with him AND his brother died AND he loves you, and that's your reconciliation text?"

"I texted him another time, too." I shrugged. "I didn't think it was so bad."

"You could have at least asked him how he was doing."

"That was implied," I explained.

"I fail to see where that implication was."

"Now I'm on *CSI*? I said hi. No one ever bothers with that in a text."

"Now I see. How could I have missed all the concern and love hidden in those two little letters?" Becca started laughing, which started her coughing.

"You totally deserve that cough. The text wasn't that bad." I scowled.

"You're right." She sipped from a cup near her bed, and her

cough eventually subsided. "You could have asked, 'How's your dead brother?'"

"If I'm that awful, why are you even friends with me?" I stood up, hurt by the implication of my coldness.

"Hey, Alex, sorry. You don't usually seem to care about being a coldhearted bitch."

"Not making this better," I noted.

"That's where so much of your charm is, Alex. It's one of the reasons I love you. And probably why Leo does—" I glanced hard at her. "Did. Maybe. Well, he *liked* you at least, right?"

"I guess," I conceded.

Could he ever again? Was that what I wanted?

A text buzzed on my phone. Becca and I locked eyes. "Open it!" she prodded.

It was a reply from Leo. One word.

Going

"What the fuck does that mean? Was he planning on writing more and sent it by accident?" I shook my phone, willing it to spit out extra words.

"I think it means he's going," Becca suggested.

"He didn't say anything about seeing me."

"He didn't say anything about your thoughtful use of the word 'hi' either. Maybe he was in a hurry."

"Maybe he was in the middle of fucking some other girl." My brain went to a terrible place.

"Alex, I'm sure he wouldn't stop having sex just to answer your text. And besides, the two of you were never just fucking."

"I don't feel any better," I admitted.

"He bothered to write you back. That's something."

"You're reaching, Becca."

"Maybe. But what's wrong with that? If we don't reach for things, think of how much we'll miss."

Then Becca fell asleep.

Her words were generically profound, like a Hallmark card I'd skim over to get to the check. But they made sense, too. How far I was willing to reach for Leo, I just didn't know yet.

CHAPTER

31

THE WEEK LEADING UP to Dead of Winter Con, Becca was up and down. Radiation every morning at 6:30, then she pushed herself to go to school. She said she wanted to feel normal, which I got and I didn't. She was hardly normal, with her fuzzy hair and extra-special treatment from everyone around her. But it had been months of bed rest, puke, and pajamas, making school a diversion. Wednesday I was supposed to drive her home, but she had to be picked up early by her mom. Becca fell asleep on her desk in French class. Her teacher let her sleep the entire time. I was surprised at how kind everyone was to Becca. So many shitty things happen to so many people; somehow cancer is the thing that made other people change their behavior. Maybe it was that Becca's illness had been so visible; not only in her diminished physical appearance, but in the gaping hole of her absence, too. I quelled the bit of jealousy I had, trying not to remember how few people acknowledged my dad's death when I came back to school after the summer.

Becca stayed home the rest of the week by order of her mom,

who gave her the choice of going to school or Dead of Winter Con. She also offered her a home visit from Rabbi Schulman, but Becca feigned a headache to get out of it. Her mom had been spending a hell of a lot of time with Rabbi Schulman. Becca didn't mind, since it meant her mom was out of her (minuscule) hair and Caleb could homeschool Becca on all kinds of matters. It pissed me off, though, that her mom would be gone so much. What if Becca were to die? And her mom missed out on all of that time with her, just to ask God that she live? Nothing made sense.

Thursday afternoon, I received a text from Becca.

#22 completed

Becca took a bath at someone else's house.

So you're breaking and entering, I texted.

Is that what we're calling it now? ;) Caleb's house has very small bathtubs, FYI.

I wanted to be happy for Becca, as jazzed about her sexual exploits as she always was for mine. But did that mean my time with the list was over? That she didn't need me anymore? If she didn't, who did?

Try not to get stuck, I texted, and tried to laugh at the possibilities of misinterpretation. But nothing felt funny when I was laughing at it alone.

Friday morning, I made another Fuck-It List attempt.

Today is #20.
You're dressed like a prostitute?
Yes.
How?

I'm wearing hoop earrings.

Whore.

At lunchtime, I wasn't in the mood for the ultra-vapid conversation, so I took my hot pretzel and Coke and snuck my way down the quiet halls.

Pulling my key ring out of my pocket, I gingerly inserted the key Leo had given me, my first and only present from him. The door to the book closet clicked open, and I entered the forbidden space.

It was a shithole.

The last time I had been there was after Leo's brother's funeral, and I had managed to nicely destroy any semblance of order the room held. I picked up the first book my shoe hit.

Fahrenheit 451.

I reached over and placed it on a shelf.

One down, thirty trillion to go.

I worked this way through the lunch hour, then, upon hearing the bell ring and the hallway fill with students, decided to stay through art. Then calculus and history.

When the bell rang signaling the end of the day, I continued to work. I felt like Bastian, up in the attic of his school in *The NeverEnding Story*. If only I had a sandwich to nibble on, so I could say to myself, "No. Not too much. We still have a long way to go. . . ."

The floor was cleared and the shelves filled around six o'clock. I felt not only a sense of accomplishment, but that somehow putting this room back together signified something great. Not great meaning good, but great in that there were possibilities. Even good ones. Which was new to me and scarier than the prospect of living on top of an Indian burial ground.

CHAPTER

BECCA HAD A BREAK from radiation for the weekend, and she was determined not to let her wobbly legs stop her from achieving her butt-touching dreams.

"The plan is," she explained on the drive to Dead of Winter Con, "we scope out the joint first. Get the lay of the land. We'll find Jamie Bamber's booth, see how long his lines are, and assess the most optimum time for an autograph. When that time comes, I'll play up the cancer angle and lure him out from behind his table for a close-encounter picture. Then, while you pretend you don't know how to work my camera, I'll put my hand on his butt."

"Why do I have to pretend that I can't work a camera?"

"It adds tension. It's how I envisioned it." Becca vibrated with excitement in her bubblegum pink wig.

"I hope you don't freak him out," Becca added, looking me over. I woke up extra early to ensure my blood was distributed in a grotesque, yet natural, fashion.

"Me freak him out? This is expected. It's a horror convention. I'm not the one grabbing genitalia."

"I'm not grabbing genitalia! Butts are not genitalia!"

"Calm down. I just wanted to use the word. I didn't know you'd have an aneurysm over it."

Speaking of aneurysms, I also spent a good portion of the morning and previous night pre-enacting scenarios of running into Leo. What if he ignored me? Pretended he didn't know who I was?

What if he was with another girl?

We arrived at the convention center and followed the herd of costumed kindred spirits into the hall. The walls were lined with vendors selling everything from bootlegged DVDs to homemade dead babies. D-level celebrities with huge, fake boobs attempted to lure lonely fanboys in for a photo and fifty-dollar autograph. We watched a twenty-something girl break down crying after meeting the star of *Gremlins*. The place was a freak show, and I reveled in it. The spirit of horror filled me, and I immediately plunked down forty dollars for a *Children of the Corn* DVD, signed by Malachai himself. "You were totally scary," I told him. He thanked me, although as I walked off I wondered if that was a compliment. He was mostly scary because of how naturally creepy-looking he was.

Becca's mom asked me to watch over her, make sure she sat down to rest even before she needed to. We made a habit of popping a squat at every corner of the hall, where others congregated to sift through their swag. People-watching at cons was one of my favorite parts of the experience. Grown men who spent their days as personal bankers changed into Rick Grimes and Freddy Krueger. Mild-mannered secretaries shed their clothes and showed off their stretch marks to the world. Nobody judged. My favorite costume at the con was a man wearing a psycho rubber baby mask, a tiny t-shirt, and a giant diaper, his hairy legs and oversized white gym shoes adding to the dementedness. I had Becca take a picture for my Facebook profile, and we moved on to the Fuck-It List quest.

No Leo sightings yet.

Jamie Bamber's booth was in a row amid other actors from horror and sci-fi TV shows. I usually had to look at the signs behind them to figure out who they were, if I recognized them at all. Jamie looked different from the military Apollo, even after his character turned into a politician and wore a pin-striped suit and longer hair. Bamber's con hair was wild and outgrown, as though to prove to the world that he was nothing like his somewhat tight-assed TV character. Of course, that show ended years ago, so maybe he grew his hair out for a role. I always wondered what it was like for actors signing at cons; was it a happy occasion, greeting fans, or did they feel pathetic in some way that their fame was stuck in a past life? What if I made one horror film that everyone loved, and then a bunch of movies most people hated? Would I be okay, signing Blu-ray covers at horror conventions, only to be remembered for my single triumph? Hell yeah, I would. It's better than not being remembered at all.

We camped out on a floor spot with optimum Bamber vision and pulled out the snacks Becca's mom forced us to bring. Becca was so enchanted with Jamie Bamber that she missed her mouth every time she attempted to insert a pretzel stick. "He's cute, right? Definitely not Fat Apollo." Bamber looked to be in excellent shape, wearing a t-shirt that showed off his efforts at the gym. "Why is his line so short?" Becca's eyes remained fixed on Bamber.

"Chewbacca's next to him. That's hard to compete with. Plus, Chewbacca's like two feet taller than him." One thing you learned going to cons is that most celebrities, unless they were playing a Wookie, were much shorter than they appeared on screen.

"When there are two people in line, we'll go." I was about to ask her how she chose that arbitrarily small number, but she sprung into action mode instantly and announced, "Two! There are two! It's go time!" I helped her off the floor, and she adjusted her wig and I ♥ Fat Apollo t-shirt before we stepped into his line. Becca gripped my hand as we waited and watched him smile for the fans in front of us. He looked rather darling, and I was sucked in, thinking of the countless hours I'd spent watching him on TV. Soon it was our turn, and I was glad this was Becca's show. She deserved something this great in her life. Becca strode right up to Bamber's table, and drew his attention to her shirt with a flourish of her hands.

"I will never live that down," he laughed. I had completely forgotten he was British.

"You do an amazing American accent," I told him as Becca fished some money out of her wallet. Another hilarious aspect of cons was how you were talking to someone you admired, but at the same time you had to ask them how much money it cost to pay for their autograph. Jamie was smart and had a handler to take the money. Some celebrities were alone at their booths and looked mortified every time they had to interrupt a gushing fan to collect cash. I stood back and let Becca charm him with her crazy fangirl chatter. He politely smiled and said things to make her laugh. When it came time for the picture, it was Jamie who asked if Becca wanted him to come around his table. Some celebrities would only lean over a table, so the pictures turned out to be you leaning backward against a table with a celebrity torso next to you. The cool ones came out, put their arms over your shoulders and acted like your best friend for thirty seconds. I played my part of bumbling photographer. "Is this where I press?" I asked, like a ninety-year-old woman. Becca took her cue, and I watched as she slowly, subtly moved her hand into position. "One, two, three!" I cried, and just as the picture snapped, Becca offered her hand on Jamie Bamber's ass.

"Whoa!" He jumped forward. I took picture after ass-groping picture to capture the hilarity of the moment. Stunned but not angry, Jamie looked at her in a jokingly scolding manner.

Becca gave her sweetest grin and told him, "Sorry! I have cancer and just had to do that." He looked confused, so she rambled on, "I wrote this bucket list, but we called it the Fuck-It List, and one of the things on it was to touch your butt and I never really thought I'd have the chance to do it especially because I got cancer but then you were here and I'm in radiation now and thank you—" I pulled her away as she finished. "You have a really solid butt!"

Jamie, ever the British gentleman, nodded a "you're welcome," and we ran off. I was laughing so hard that I didn't realize Becca sat down to rest somewhere behind me. I stopped walking and turned around to sit with her. Together, we panted and laughed and flipped through the pictures to relive the moment we just had. I hadn't noticed that two Chuck-wearing feet approached me until someone tapped my heel with his. I looked up, and there was Leo.

CHAPTER

33

"HEY." *LEO NUDGED* my shoe. I stood up so his towering height was a bit less towering. Not seeing him for so long, I thought I was over the magnetic quality his body had with mine. Not so much. He looked really good. "You shaved your head," I noted, and reached up to feel it. He only slightly recoiled.

"We match." Becca smiled. Leo forcibly smiled back.

"I'm Brian, by the way. Thanks for introducing me, bro." Leo's friend extended a hand for me to shake, then down to Becca. He didn't go to our school, but I had seen him with Leo once or twice on stalking expeditions. And Jason's funeral. He wore a slight pompadour in his dyed black hair and carried a friendly rockabilly vibe.

"That's a good look for you." Leo reached for my face, and it took me a melty second to realize he was talking about my fake blood. He touched a dangling bit of flesh, but none of my own. I smelled cigarettes on his hand.

"Thanks. It's not real, in case you were worried," I told him.

"Worry about you? I'm sure you can handle yourself," Leo quipped. I didn't know if he thought that was a good or bad thing.

"Did you guys go to any panels?" asked Brian. The conversation turned lighthearted, or as lighthearted as one can get when talking about *Deathbox 4*. I tried to stop myself from staring at Leo. Had he really said he loved me once? Where would we be now if his brother hadn't died? If Becca didn't have cancer? If my dad hadn't died? Would he have stayed a distant object of my imagination? Tragedy is what brought us together. And then pushed us apart.

Where were we now?

I've heard countless people say bad things happen in threes. That never made sense to me. Shit happened all the time; how could anybody determine where the pattern of three ended and the next one began? Maybe Leo's brother dying had nothing to do with my first two bad things. Maybe Becca was going to die. Or my mom. Or one of my brothers. Or both. If both of them died, did that count as one or two bad things?

No, I didn't believe in the "cycle of three bad things" any more than I believed in love at first sight and giving people the benefit of the doubt. Love was never going to be something you could find in the split-second glance of judgment we make on people we don't know, and if people seemed like they were up to no good, chances are they were. My dad taught me that.

Just because three horrible things happened, that didn't mean more weren't to come. Better to protect yourself than kick yourself later for being an asshole. Now, that was something I believed in.

"Can someone help me up?" Becca asked, and before I could reach for her, Brian extended his hand. While they made with the niceties, Leo and I looked at each other, on the verge of words. I must have opened my mouth five times while trying to think of something to say. We looked like two fish in an aquarium.

I studied Leo's face, the straight lips, the too-sweet freckles, his translucent eyelashes. In that moment I hated myself for not trying to be there for him.

Fish mouth again.

Brian broke the underwater moment. "You guys want to come to the screening of *Reanimator* with us?"

"I'm sure they're busy," Leo informed him.

"Yeah," I agreed out of obligation. "We can't. I promised Becca's mom I'd bring her home for dinner. She's hardcore about making her eat her vegetables." I looked at Becca, whose mom told her to stay out as long as she wanted.

"Yeah." She presented her best disappointed face, always the actress. "Maybe another time?" she asked.

"Sure." Brian smiled, googly eyed. If he only knew Becca was attached to a homeschool beefcake.

Not knowing how to say good-bye, nor really wanting to, I blurted, "Want to get coffee sometime?" at Leo, a line direct from the list of top asshole-isms.

"Maybe," Leo answered, kind of sounding like an asshole himself.

"That would be great," Becca pushed. That he would *maybe* want to get coffee with me? I felt like I was morphing into one gigantic asshole as we spoke. Like, literally a human-sized hole in an ass.

"Better get in line so we can get seats. Nice meeting you guys." Brian winked. I always said never trust a winker.

Or anyone else for that matter.

Leo and Brian walked away, and Becca and I headed for my car. "What happened?" she asked.

"What do you mean?" I played dumb. Or maybe I just was.

"That was your big chance to charm Leo back into your evil clutches, and you totally choked."

"I didn't choke. He didn't want to see me. Or watch *Reanimator* with me. Or drink hot caffeinated beverages with me." I stomped ahead of Becca, who called after me, "Slow down!"

I stopped and waited for her to catch up. "I need to sit down," she said. We plopped down on a parking block, so Becca could rest.

"I fucked this up, didn't I? Not just today, but, like, forever."

"Possibly not. Leo did say maybe. He could have flat-out said no and called you a twat."

"Leo has never used the word 'twat'," I guessed.

"Well, more people should."

"Do you think I'm a twat?"

"Not all the time." I flicked Becca's arm. "Watch it. I bruise easily. What I meant was, maybe you are a twat sometimes, but Leo already knew that. Maybe he understands. I mean, you just lost your dad, and then his brother goes and dies. People deal with death in all sorts of weird ways."

"Really? I hadn't noticed, Davis Humper."

"Did you seriously just use the word 'hump'?"

"Don't forget Davis."

"Wish I could."

That night, as I replayed every detail of my debacle with Leo, my phone buzzed on my nightstand. It was a text. From Leo.

Yes to coffee. Tomorrow?

Fuckbaskets. What made him change his mind? Was this his opportunity to tell me off? To make up? To introduce me to his fiancée?

I didn't want to wait and give him a chance to change his mind.

Have to work tomorrow.
After work
OK. 7:30 @ Brew Town?
OK

I waited for more texts, felt like I should say something else but lacked the words to express anything. What would I express if I had? I wished my mom had homeschooled me, so I had the gall to write sappy love notes like Caleb. But Leo wasn't the sappy love-note type. I didn't think. Whether or not he was, I wasn't. I couldn't even handle those three little words.

I handled liking the guy who said them even less.

CHAPTER

I WAS A JANGLY BALL of stress all day at Cellar. Too many hunks of turkey and plops of mayonnaise missed their bread, and my feet were surrounded by casualties.

"Are you on the rag or something?" accused Doug. "You're surlier than ever today."

"Maybe. Want me to pull out my bloody tampon and show you?" That shut him up. Guys seemed much better equipped at handling the hypothetically hormonal aspect of menstruation than the actual act.

My shift ended at seven. Brew Town was only two stores away, and I used the extra half hour to change out of my subby shirt and into one that didn't smell quite as much like roast beef. At 7:25, I ascended the stairs and walked out the door of Cellar. There, two doors down, leaning against the storefront with a cigarette in his hand, was Leo.

He wore a heavy black down jacket and a black winter hat over his buzzed hair. He looked around nonchalantly, either not in a rush to find me or really just taking in the sights. When our eyes met, he brought the cigarette to his lips, took a long drag, blew out the smoke, then stamped out the rest of the cigarette with his shoe. It could have been a calculated move to show me that he was smoking again, that I had no influence over him. Or maybe he started smoking again because of other reasons. Because the world was oh-so-far from revolving around me.

I approached Leo, and he eased himself out of his window lean.

"Hey," I said.

"Hey," he repeated. He held the door open for me with his back, hands in his pockets. Without taking off his coat, he slid into a table near the window.

"What do you want?" I asked, standing next to him. He looked at me, almost annoyed. "Coffee?" I pushed.

"Oh. Large. Black."

I didn't bother asking him which brew. I guessed that wasn't something he cared much about. At the counter, I ordered him a medium roast and hoped it was the right choice. I selected a mocha for myself. When the barista asked for the name on my order, I told him, "Ash," the name of Bruce Campbell's character in the Evil Dead movies. I thought maybe it would soften the situation. I waited by the counter for the drinks, and when the barista called, "Ash," I looked over at Leo for approval. He watched passersby at the window. I was pissed at myself for bothering.

"Your black coffee." I delivered the cup in front of Leo, drawing his attention back inside. I shook off my coat but left on my gloves, fingerless ones that converted into mittens.

"Thanks," Leo offered flatly, and poured a heaping amount of sugar into his cup.

I felt like I was supposed to talk. But what about? The easiest segue into conversation was Dead of Winter Con, so I took it.

"How was *Reanimator?*"

"The same as it always is." Leo didn't look at me when he answered.

He stirred his coffee. I blew on mine. An imaginary clock ticked loudly in my brain.

"Why are we here?" I broke the silence. He managed to look at me. I wanted to drown in his green eyes, until he said, "Fuck if I know. Brian made me text you last night."

"He made you? Like, held a gun to your head and threatened your firstborn?"

Leo stared at me drolly. "This was your idea. Total mistake." He abruptly pushed his chair back but didn't stand.

"I don't feel like it is," I told him.

"What do you feel, Alex?"

Shit. Was this the moment where I was supposed to excrete emotions? Was that the only way to make this thing right?

"Do you still love me?" I asked.

Wrong question.

"Seriously. Seriously? You are royally fucked up, Alex."

"Oh, is that why you asked me here? To be a total dick and tell me shitty things about myself? Because I don't need you for that. Perfectly capable of self-loathing on my own, thank you."

We stared at each other through squinted eyes. If we were bulls, steam would have come snorting out of our noses.

"Why did you ask me here? And don't tell me because Brian made you."

"I don't know. It's been a shitty few months, and as much as I hated running into you yesterday you looked really cute with that viscera hanging off your head."

And . . . melt.

I tried not to smile at the compliment, but it was impossible not to. "That's a good word. Viscera."

"Yeah," he agreed. We watched each other, silent again, less snorty. "I need more than cute viscera, though." He sipped his coffee.

"Like what?" I asked, stumped.

"I'm not going to feed you your lines, Alex." I still didn't know what to say. He waited. "So that's it, then?" he questioned.

Part of me had hoped that everything that happened, or didn't happen, in the last few months could be erased. Forgotten. What good would it do to rehash all of the shit?

I'm the idiot who asked if he still loved me. And I'm also the idiot who decided to say, "I got a new print of *Children of the Corn* if you want to watch it."

"Maybe." He didn't look quite as mad anymore, just disappointed. Which was much worse.

I stood up and walked over to his chair. We were about the same height when he sat and I stood, and I pulled off his hat to run my fingers over his hair. It had worked for me in the past when words failed me, as they often did. I leaned in and stole a kiss, then backed away to gauge his reaction. He grabbed my wrist and pulled me toward him, his other hand cupping my neck as he kissed me back. The warmth rushed from my lips to my toes, and for a minute all was forgiven.

Until he pushed me away and snatched back his hat. "Damnit, Alex." He wiped his lips off with the top of his hand. "I gotta go." He crushed his hat back on his head and shoved his way out the door, leaving his large coffee behind.

I slunk back to my chair and sipped my mocha. When I was done, I forced myself to drink the rest of Leo's coffee, too. The bitter taste filled my mouth and coated my stomach. I imagined it was poison, a concoction that would eat away at my tongue, my teeth, my esophagus, rendering me physically speechless. A fitting end to someone who never said the right thing.

CHAPTER

35

BECCA STAYED HOME from school much of the next week. The radiation made her throat incredibly sore, to the point where swallowing hurt. Her mom wouldn't let me come over, telling me I made Becca laugh too much and that would just hurt her throat more. I sent Becca a link to *Ordinary People*, the saddest movie ever made, with the note, "I hope you never laugh again."

She wrote me back that Caleb had come to her rescue with homemade hard candies.

Right. Hard candies. I know what you mean.

Perv.

Takes one to know one.

It was hard to communicate with Becca about Leo through typing only. She was stuck on the positive of "At least he wanted to see you. And he kissed you!"

"And then he stopped kissing me. Is there anything more mortifying than a guy not wanting to kiss you back?"

"Try not being able to kiss a guy because you have puke breath twenty-four, seven."

That shut me up. My problems still weren't real problems next to Becca's.

I drowned my sorrow and guilt in Ben and Jerry's and horror movies. Friday night, my mom asked if I would watch the twins so she could play mahjong with some friends.

"I know they're old enough to be alone, but I'd feel better if you were home with them. Please don't drive anywhere." Mom had chilled a lot with her tension over driving, except at the thought of her three children being alone in a car together. She never said, but I knew what she thought; if we were all driving together, we could all die together, too. I told her we'd stay home, order pizza, watch some movies.

"Nothing too scary," Mom requested. "CJ wouldn't want you to know, but he's been having nightmares lately."

For being such a turd, CJ sure was sensitive.

I suggested we watch *Dead Set* with our pizza. "You know how you always ask me why I dress like this everyday? Well, now you'll know. Plus, you love reality TV."

"Sounds cool," AJ agreed.

CJ wasn't so convinced. "Is it scary?"

"No. It's fake. Do you believe in zombies?"

"Not really. I mean, no." CJ played it cool.

"The show is about a group of idiots on a reality show where they all have to live together in the same house. We get to watch behind the scenes, too, which is where my character is. Then, outside the house, where they're totally locked in, the world is overrun with zombies. And they have to figure out what to do. It's genius. Way more gross than scary. You love gross, CJ. Remember that mole rat that was eating its own baby at the zoo? It's practically the same thing."

CJ was lightly convinced by the mole rat, and we started the marathon. All was well for the first hour. But then things took a turn for the worse, and not just for the characters turning into the living dead.

"Can we turn it off?" I hadn't noticed that CJ was squinting his eyes in an effort not to see the screen. I paused, unintentionally on a screen shot of someone getting their eyeball eaten.

"Just turn it off!" CJ yelled. I complied. This wasn't normal CJ behavior. Tears formed at the corners of his closed eyes.

"It's off. What's wrong? It's not real," I told him.

"But it was real! People die! And they look gross! Dad looked gross!" CJ began full-on sobbing.

I didn't know what to do. Not that I ever did, but it was paralyzing seeing my normally brash and annoying tween brother turn into a blubbering little kid. Then things got even worse. AJ began crying, too.

"What's going on?" I panicked.

"Don't you ever think about him, Alex? Don't you miss him?"

Dad. I rarely heard them talk about Dad, not in a way that expressed any sadness.

"Of course I do," I admitted.

"Then how come you never talk about him?" CJ sniffed.

"What do you want me to say? Remember when Dad got mangled in a taxi?"

Wrong again. CJ exploded like a four-year-old who lost his blankey.

"I'm sorry. I'm sorry," I fumbled. "I do miss him. I loved him so much. He was my dad. Our dad. He was funny. And smart. And he listened and taught us things and now he'll never be here to teach us anything else. Like how to make my gigantic brothers feel better when they're crying next to me on the couch." I pressed back my own tears, until AJ started laughing.

"We're not gigantic," he snuffled.

Somehow that made more tears escape from my eyes. "To me you are. You sure you guys weren't adopted?" I joked.

"You're the death-loving weirdo," CJ noted.

"I don't love death," I defended myself.

"Then why do you watch this stuff?" He waved his hand at the blackened television.

"Because it's not death. It's ridiculous. It's fake and it's controlled and it's hilarious and girls like me can kick zombie ass, that's why. Because in the movies, I could stop Dad from getting in a cab and turning into shrapnel."

AJ and CJ just looked at me. I didn't know if they got the full impact of my confession, that even making a confession was one of the hardest things I could do.

"What's shrapnel?" CJ asked.

"Never mind. That's not important." I rubbed my eyes. "You guys want to watch something else?"

"We never got to watch this week's *Wipeout*," AJ hinted.

"Big balls it is." I switched on *Wipeout*, and my heart warmed at the sight and sound of my brothers laughing at others' stupidity.

It wasn't a direct lesson from my dad, and it was about the most sour lemonade I could have made out of lemons, but his death forced me to have a real talk with my brothers for maybe the first time ever. And for the first time in forever, some of my guilt finally lifted.

That night, my mom home, the twins in bed, I sent a text to Leo.

I want to say I'm sorry, but I don't know how.

Those words, "I'm sorry," felt so contrived to me for so long and yet I knew they were important. What Leo did with them was up to him.

CHAPTER

36

SNOW FELL STEADILY on my way to work Saturday, and I gripped the steering wheel to the point of hand cramps. Drivers ed never prepared me for skidding sideways uncontrollably until my possessed car decided to stop inches from a stop sign. Not to mention how other people drove like complete assholes. I don't know how many times I yelled into my rearview mirror, "Two car lengths, dickwad!" There were very few things I feared, and driving in snow was one of them. My mom claimed it would get better with practice, but since it didn't snow year-round, how could I ever stay on top of it? I'd either have to move to Antarctica to have snow all the time or the equator to never have it. But I liked the seasons.

I arrived at work shaking and dripping in sweat.

"Did you run here?" asked Ila. She wore fingerless gloves, as the front counter received a lot of the draft from the opening door.

I peeled my scarf away from my neck and shivered at the newly exposed wetness. "Snowshoed, actually." I hung my jacket up in the back room and pulled my grungy work t-shirt out of my schoolbag. Before I re-smoothed my hair into a low ponytail and tucked a towel into my waistband, I checked my phone. No reply from Leo. Using Becca's positive thinking, I told myself he probably slept in. Using my usual apocalyptic brand of thinking, I guessed he barfed on the word "sorry" and had his phone number changed.

Since it was only 10:00 a.m., the lunch rush was still to come, although on a snowy day there could either be a ton of people who didn't want to cook or just a trickle of customers. Enough people lived within walking distance, and walking around in the snow was a lot easier than driving. I passed the time by refilling the mayo and mustard squeeze bottles, restocking cheese, and arguing with Doug about the greatest sequels of all time.

"Aside from the obvious *Evil Dead* and *Basket Case*, I think *A Nightmare on Elm Street* 3 was really good," I said.

"I haven't even seen that. I'm sure it sucks. Commercial crap."

"Aren't we all pretentious, Mr. College Student? You can't judge a movie you haven't seen. We're talking teens in a mental hospital. At one point, Freddy pulls out some kid's tendons and works him like a marionette. Brilliant."

I was so busy making my obviously winning point that it took me a few minutes to notice Leo watching me on the other side of the counter. He wore a gray winter hat this time with his black winter coat. Not that I noticed. His cheeks were red from where the falling snow burned them.

"You know nothing," I told Doug as I budged past him toward Leo. "Hey," I greeted him, hopefulness practically exploding off my face.

"Hey." He leaned on the counter, as was his usual position here. It had been so long, though, did he actually have a usual position?

"Thank you for the text," he said.

"You're welcome," I offered. It seemed like enough to start the flow of conversation.

"How's Becca doing?" He surprised me with the question, even though it was what a nice person would ask. She did have cancer, and she did once barf in his general direction.

"She's okay. Chemo is over, but she's in radiation which seems to also suck. She's really weak." I didn't like the sound of that, since Becca was trying to kick cancer's ass. "I mean, she's tough, but it's never-ending. I still don't understand why the treatment is so unbelievably cruel. She passed one hundred days. Sick for one hundred fucking days."

"Seriously? That long? I feel like this year has gone on for ten years."

That wasn't good. I was part of his extra-long year. So was his brother, I knew, but if only I had been there for him when I should have, maybe it wouldn't have felt so long.

"So how are you?" I asked. The dumbest question in the universe. Still working on moving along the conversation.

Leo shrugged, an appropriately ambiguous answer. The awful thing was that I really wanted to know how he was, and that was one of the things that kept me from talking to him since his brother's death. The longer I waited, the less we'd have to say, the more blanks no one wanted to fill in. Those blanks could be sadder than that ridiculously sad movie I sent to laughless Becca.

"How are *you*?" Leo asked back.

"Okay," I answered. "I hate this snow. I mean, I actually love it aesthetically and how quiet it makes everything at three a.m., but I'm terrified of driving in it," I admitted.

"You? Terrified of something? You're full of surprises today."

"Full of them? What else?" I asked.

"I think that might have been the first time you asked me how I am. Ever." He was serious.

"It's not because I don't want to know. It's just such a contrived question. I usually figure if someone really wants to tell me how they are they'll just tell me. No need to pull it out of them."

"You are abnormal." Leo studied me.

"Thank you," I answered dryly.

"Sometimes I think you might be a robot. Or an alien. At least genetically engineered somehow," Leo said.

"That would explain my freakish elbow dimples."

"Or how you could just stop talking to someone after what we had."

So it was time to talk about that.

"Can we go sit at a table?" I asked, noticing that the lack of customers made Leo and me center stage for my fellow sub makers.

Leo didn't answer but led the way to a table, the same table where we first sat months ago. I wished I could say life was simpler back then, but it seemed like life was never going to be simple. Maybe if we were Amish. He shrugged off his jacket and flipped it over the back of his chair, which I took as a positive sign compared to the coffee shop. His hat stayed on, probably to keep his newly shorn head warm. The hat made him look snuggly, and I had the urge to lean over and rub it. I resisted, knowing we weren't there yet, nor did I know if we would ever be again.

Leo looked at me intently, and I knew he expected me to speak. It was he who had come to my work, though, and I hadn't prepared anything. The text was a huge step for me, and I hadn't yet figured out what would follow it. I convinced myself I'd probably never hear from Leo again.

Yet here he was.

He kicked back in his chair and slung one arm over the back, his eyes never leaving my face. Feigning confidence, I continued to meet his eyes, which had the uncomfortable effect of making me want to touch him again. Even though I stopped talking to Leo, even though I totally fled when he probably needed me most, and even though I made it a point to move on with my semblance of a life, I couldn't dispute the fact that I. Liked. Leo.

Shit.

It was so much easier being with guys I didn't like. Davis went off to join the army, and I hadn't thought about him since. For all I knew, he was dead, too, right alongside Leo's brother.

Leo's brother. Right then it hit me what it could have been like if I were with someone like Leo when my dad died. I doubt he would have left me out of fear like Davis left me.

Like I left him.

"I am such an asshole," I said, not quite meaning to, aloud.

Leo didn't disagree.

"I was your Davis," I decided. "I should just go off and join the army."

"Who's Davis? And there's no way you're joining the army."

"Don't tell me what to do," I argued.

"You seriously want to join the army? All five feet of you?"

"I'm five foot two, and, well, no. I don't want to join the army. I just need to stop speaking."

"You already did that, remember?" Leo looked smug.

"What are you doing here, Leo? I have no idea what to say to you. I'm not going to apologize anymore because I did that and apologies are really just bullshit to make the apologizer feel better. And I don't deserve to feel better. I should feel like absolute, total shit. I deserve someone to take out my tendons and parade me around like a marionette."

"Diarrhea mouth, can you plug it for a second?"

The thought of having plugged diarrhea in my mouth shut me up.

"I'm not looking for another apology—" Leo started, but I cut him off.

"I don't know what to give you. I have nothing to say that will make anything better. Nothing is going to bring Jason back, and it's totally my fault." Wait. What?

"Alex, how could Jason's death be your fault?" Leo unhooked his arm from the chair and put his hand on the table near mine, but not touching.

"I don't think I meant that. I mean, of course I didn't." I picked at a jagged fingernail.

"Do you think your dad's death was your fault?"

"No," I argued. "But I just don't get it. Any of it. I don't want any more real horror in my life. There's nothing funny about actual death and disease. If only my dad could come back because of a rabid monkey at the zoo." I laughed to myself at the ridiculous horror movie sentiment.

"Or as a reanimated prostitute," Leo added.

"Maybe we should have buried them in pet cemeteries," I suggested.

"That never ends well," Leo admitted. I had never joked about my dad's death with someone, not someone who had a death of their own to joke about.

"Do you believe things happen for a reason?" Leo brought the conversation back to serious.

"No," I answered emphatically.

"Me neither," he concurred. "I can't buy the idea that we're supposed to live and learn from horrible things. That somehow these things happen so we can grow as people."

"I hope nothing else happens to you," I told him, "because you have done enough growing." I held my hand over my head acknowledging his exceptional height.

"Maybe that's why shit *does* keep happening to you. Because you need to grow. Shorty."

"That was quite possibly the lamest insult anyone has ever bestowed upon me."

"Forgive me. I'm out of practice. Being away from everyone except your depressed parents will do that to you."

"That sucks," I said. "You should come back to school. Better of two evils? I'm there." I prodded.

"So that would make school the bigger of two evils." Leo smiled, and one of his fingers stroked one of mine. My toes wiggled.

"Alex! A little help here!" I hadn't noticed that the snowy eaters had arrived, and a line was backing up.

"I guess I have to go work." I rolled my eyes.

"That is what they pay you for." Leo stood as I did.

"I thought it was for my bubbly personality and smaller-than-average butt."

"Imagine the tips if you had an even average-sized butt."

"You're lucky I still feel guilty, or I might have to hit you." I started walking behind the counter.

Leo grabbed my arm. "No more guilt, okay?"

I nodded weakly. Guilt was the one thing I'd held on to for everyone. "So you're saying I shouldn't blame myself for you smoking again?" I raised an eyebrow.

"Let's say you were a coconspirator, but I was the mastermind."

"I can live with that."

"Good."

"Alex!" Doug yelled again. "I need more meat!"

"Should I be jealous?" Leo asked.

"I wouldn't mind if you were." I almost felt coquettish, if such a thing were possible. We both smiled.

"Alex! Meat! Now!" Doug harassed me.

"Better go give Doug his meat. See you in school?" I suggested. "There's a book closet that misses you terribly."

Leo pulled a chain out from his shirt that hung around his neck and held it up for me to see. I recognized a familiar-looking key and the distinctive shape of dog tags. He tucked the chain back in, gave a small wave and a smile, and walked up the stairs.

I felt really good. And it scared me.

CHAPTER

37

NO LEO THE REST of the week at school, nor the entire next week. We started texting, benign conversations about movies on *Svengoolie*. I subtly tried to coax him back to school, but I was afraid to push it.

> **They're threatening to start construction on the book closet wing if you don't show up.**
> **Nice try. That's not scheduled until next year.**
> **I might knock it down myself then.**
> **That I'd come to see.**

But the days passed, and that was as much contact as we had. I started to believe I imagined our Cellar visit, residual brain fog from Becca's pot smoke. She was having a particularly nauseous time from the radiation combined with the sore throat. I did my best to cheer her up with visits and pints of ice cream, but it didn't feel like enough. It never did.

Becca's mom was in a particularly dark, religious state. Every moment she could get away from the house, she did. Sometimes it was shopping, sometimes spa days, but she spent most of her time at the synagogue. On the rare occasion I did see her, I wished I hadn't. One afternoon, when Becca seemed to ache in the most random places, her mom walked in with a grossly pained expression. I think Becca's cancer installed at least six new worry wrinkles on her mom's face. She tutted, clicked her tongue, made all sorts of exaggeratedly worrisome sounds as she watched Becca on her bed. Under her breath, I heard her say, "God will see you through." Then she left again. Unsettling.

"What is up with your mom?" I asked, taking over game duty from Becca. She liked to think of herself as my sensei to the world of RPGs, and I complied as long as she agreed to watch *Waxwork I* and *II* with me. I bought the set with some birthday money from Aunt Judy.

"She's like the prophet of doom." Becca's voice was quiet and scratchy, but her head was together. I liked that. "She thinks it's a bad sign that I'm so sick, even though I'm done with chemo."

"She told you that?"

"I speak crazy mom clicks."

"You don't think it means anything, do you?"

"Who knows? I never thought about having cancer in the first place, and here I am. We still have to wait a month to find out if destroying my body also just happened to destroy the cancer."

"It fucking better have."

"You tell that cancer, Alex. Maybe you'll scare it out of me."

If only.

Friday afternoon I came home to an empty house and plopped myself in front of the TV. No Leo, Becca in limbo, and I was in a bad head space. As I flipped through the channels, it all seemed so pointless. Why were brainless people followed around all day with cameras, and why did people watch them? Why did singers spend millions of dollars on one stupid video for one shitty song when there was still no cure for cancer? Why were so many assholes all over the news and reality television and on sports teams and so many good people were dead?

And where did I fall in all of it?

My dream, to make horror movies, was so pointless. What good did it do for anyone? Who did it help? Nothing I did ever helped anyone. I couldn't stop my dad or Leo's brother from dying. I couldn't stop Becca from getting cancer. She could still die. My mom could die. My brothers. What if there were a zombie attack, and I was the last person left on Earth? Everyone dying around me, everyone becoming the undead, and I was the only one left living?

When my mom and brothers came home, I sat comatose on the couch, staring forward at nothing after the TV finally sickened me to the point of turning it off.

CJ, always the turd, saw me and asked, "Who died?" AJ smacked him in the back of the head, but CJ just asked him an incredulous, "What?" I guess we were related.

"Your fucking dad died, remember?" I asked coldly.

"Alex!" my mom scolded.

"Did you hear what he said, Mom?"

"It's just an expression. Tone it down," CJ said.

In a second I was on him, smacking CJ in the face and slamming my fist into his shoulder. I don't remember the last time I hit one of my little brothers, since they had passed the point of being little and outgrew me by at least five inches. CJ was an athlete, and while I may be scrappy, he outweighed me by thirty pounds of muscle. Somehow he had me pinned to the ground in seconds.

"What? Are you on the wrestling team? All you need now is a lobotomy and some tights." I quoted *The Breakfast Club* into the carpet.

My mom came to my rescue, although I wouldn't have minded before my brother's knee wedged into my back. "CJ, get off your sister. Boys, up to your room. Your sister and I need to talk."

"Why are we the ones in trouble? She started it." CJ pouted as he huffed up the stairs.

"You're not in trouble. You have a computer in your room, and that's where you would have gone anyway to play *Blood and Bones 12* or whatever horrific game it is you boys are into now."

My mom helped me off the ground. We sat on the couch and waited for the twins' bedroom door to slam before Mom started talking. "I know you're having a hard time, honey—"

"That's the thing. I'm not having a hard time. I'm still alive. I'm still healthy. It's everyone around me that horrible things are happening to. And I feel guilty every second of every day because I can't do a thing about it."

"Hold on. You think because you're alive, because you're not sick, that nothing is happening to you? Oh, honey. That's just not true. You're allowed to have feelings, you know. Your dad is gone. I cry about that every single day because he was my husband, the father of my wonderful children." She stroked my cheek. "And I loved him so much. Do you think I shouldn't be upset because I'm not the dead one?"

I shook my head.

"And Becca, of course you feel bad. It's almost harder for those who love the person who is sick because, you're right, there's not a whole lot you can do. Except what you are doing: being there for her. You have to stop thinking you're supposed to be so tough all the time."

"I don't think I'm tough!" I was appalled by how dorky that sounded.

"You know what I mean. You have such an emotional wall up. Like, if you let it down that means you're weak."

I hated to admit she was right because it sounded ridiculous, but I did hate the idea of being weak. The stupid girl in the horror movie who hid from the killer instead of fighting back. The screaming idiot who went up the stairs instead of to their car and away from the scene. In a way, I knew it was one of the reasons I watched horror movies; it gave me a feeling of moral superiority. But in real life, there was no obvious bad guy for me to slay, no ending where the dead person came back to life.

"I feel useless," I admitted to my mom. "Nothing I do is important."

"Now that's bullshit." My mom surprised me with her swear, usually reserved for driving. "You want me to make you a list?" Mom didn't wait for an answer and started ticking things off with her fingers. "You help keep this family together. You have a job and make money instead of sitting on the couch. You make people laugh. You're mostly nice to your brothers who need a big sister more than ever now. Your grades are good. And you are a wonderful friend through thick and thin. And someday"—Mom cleared her throat, as if this were hard for her to admit—"you will be an incredible filmmaker."

"I thought you didn't want me to make movies. That it wasn't practical. And you were totally right."

"No, I wasn't. If it will make you happy and fulfilled, then it is practical."

"But it's so pointless. Horror movies don't help anyone."

But right when I said it, I knew I was wrong. Horror movies could help people, just as they helped me. I don't know how I could have made it through the last summer without their mindless gore to keep my thoughts off my life. The conventions and all of the people who shared their love of horror. And Leo. Without horror movies, I didn't know what would have brought us together.

"You are a wonderful person, Alex. A little dark, maybe," Mom laughed. "Don't beat yourself up. You've got two brothers who can do that now."

"Yeah. When did that happen?"

Mom kissed my forehead. "I love you very much."

"Love you, too," I mumbled, and Mom went to the kitchen to make dinner. I pulled my cell phone out of my pocket and sent two texts. The first was to Becca.

Want me to come over tonight? Buffy marathon on Logo.

The second was to Leo.

I've been waiting in the book closet for 2 weeks. Starting to get hungry. Where are u?

Maybe it wasn't overly emotional, but whatever it was, it was time to stop kicking myself for it.

CHAPTER

38

I DIDN'T EXPECT to hear back from Leo. I thought, and hoped, that Monday would come and there he'd appear in the hallway asking me to smoke a cigarette as if he had never left.

Later Friday night, while Becca slept in her bed next to me as I watched the Master break Buffy's neck in a parallel world, my phone buzzed.

If you can get out of the closet, want to come over?

It was only eight, but Becca had crashed early from her pain meds. I liked to be around in case she woke up and wanted a glass of water or a note thrown at Caleb's window. But Leo wanted to see me. And I wanted to see Leo. Leaving Sleeping Baldy didn't make me a bad friend. Plus, visiting Leo when he wanted me to made me a good friend. Or at least an okay one.

I texted him back.

Yes. Rabid Grannies?

Definitely.

Rabid Grannies was an oddly dubbed Dutch movie, odd because some-times it actually looked like the actors were mouthing what they were saying in English. I always said I'd learn Dutch just to figure out what the hell was going on. Maybe I could put that on my bucket list, if I ever made one. It wasn't any less noble than prank calls and masturbation.

I gingerly slipped out of the bed and put on my shoes. "Becca," I whispered. "Becca." She stirred enough to roll over but only responded by way of a snore. I found a Post-it on her desk and scrawled, "Went to Leo's. Will let you know what happens when you stop snoring." I stuck it to her pillow.

The crud of February had set in. All along the side of the road sat piles of mucky snow, hardened and blackened from the toxic sludge of cars. At least it wasn't scary to drive in.

I pulled my winter hat as far over my ears as it could go and I tucked my gloved hands into my down jacket. The temperature had to be in the zeroes, which meant frozen boogers and cracking hair if I didn't have time to dry it. I let my car warm up for two minutes, as was the advice of my dad when he taught me to drive. The worst part was having to sit in a frigid car until the little temperature gauge showed signs of life. Until then, turning on the heat only pulled freezing air away from the freezing motor.

When I saw the hint of temperature gauge movement, I turned the heat on full blast and put the car in gear. Before I went to Leo's, I stopped at home to get the DVD. Mom sat on the couch with a tissue, blowing her nose and wiping tears from her eyes.

I had the most selfish thought of disappointment, that if my mom was crying I'd have to put my visit with Leo on hold to console her. But when she saw me, she pointed to a black-and-white movie on the TV. "Bogey and Bacall," she sniffed. "One of my favorites." I kicked myself with relief that she was only crying over a movie and ran upstairs to my room for the DVD.

"Forgot this." I held up the movie, and she acknowledged with a wave of her hankie. I didn't feel the need to explain where I was bringing the movie, and I'd still be home by eleven thirty as expected.

When I pulled up to Leo's, I took a minute in the car to think about what might happen. The last time I was there, his brother had just died. We had sex. He said he loved me. This time I was packing an imported DVD called *Rabid Grannies*.

I rang the doorbell, and to my surprise his mom answered. I had only been at Leo's one time before when his parents were also there, and they left soon after I arrived. I fumbled with my words, not knowing whether to bring up Jason or acknowledge how long it had been since I'd seen her. "Hi," was all that came out of my mouth, and I spent an inordinate amount of time wiping the wet off my shoes. I heard the pound of Leo's feet down the stairs, and he said, "Thanks, Mom. I didn't hear the doorbell." His mom said nothing and somberly shuffled away in her slippers.

"Sorry," he said as he took my coat and hung it on the end of the banister. "My mom's moods alternate between comatose and falsely perky these days."

"That was the perky one, right?" I asked. He smiled a small smile, the kind he made that first day we hung out at the elementary school.

"I hope it's okay if we watch in my room. Mom and Dad commandeered the big screen. I have a shitty setup, but it works."

"Sure." I shrugged. "The DVD looks like crap anyway, so it will be extra crispy."

"Crispy?" he asked as we walked up the stairs.

"And Dutch."

His bedroom window had been replaced, and his room was relatively neat compared to the last time I was up there. As I popped the DVD into his player, Leo lay down on his bed. There was a desk chair, and I considered sitting in it but thought that would be uncool. He was already on the bed, and it offered the best view of the TV. I lay down next to him, careful not to touch. He didn't make any move to get closer. We started the movie, and my back, rigid with tension, eventually softened as the grotesque cast of characters began their journey to their great aunt's house to find out which greedy soul inherited the fortune. Leo and I laughed at the dub and tried to figure out what the Dutch words for "eat" and "bludgeon" were. At some point, maybe halfway through, Leo's arm connected with mine. A laugh moved it there, but he didn't move it away after the laugh stopped. I inhaled involuntarily and hoped he didn't notice. I had on a short-sleeved shirt, he had on long sleeves. Maybe he couldn't even tell we were touching.

As the movie ended, we weakly applauded. "How did you ever manage to live without experiencing the pleasure of *Rabid Grannies?*" I asked.

He answered with a kiss. It was a firm kiss, and he held my cheek with one large hand. I needed that kiss. Every part of me needed it. Not just my body, which screamed at me to touch him ever since I landed on his bed again, but my mind, my heart, my soul. I needed him to show me he forgave me wholly for leaving him, so that I could show Leo how I truly felt for him.

For minutes, it was kissing, hands everywhere, clothes still on. It was me who wriggled my hand underneath Leo's shirt.

"Wait." He stopped me. "I don't want to have sex."

I had said it to him before, more than once, but hearing it said to me made me feel unwanted.

"Why not?" I asked, peeved. I didn't know if I was mentally ready to go at it again with Leo, but I was afraid to hear why he didn't want to do it with me.

I sat up and crossed my arms over my chest as though my body was somehow exposed through my black t-shirt.

"Don't get mad," he told me. "I'm just not ready to go there again yet. We've barely talked in months, and I can't pretend we're starting where we left off. I mean, shit, you dumped my ass where we left off."

"I was hoping you forgot about that," I said. "Maybe if we had sex you would?" I smiled at him through a cheesy grin.

"Momentarily, I'm sure I would. But, and stop me if you don't feel this way at all, I'm kind of wanting something more than sex and gore with you."

I hid "sex and gore" away in my brain as a kickass name for a movie. "No," I said coyly, or as coy as I could muster. "I don't just want that either. I think I *did* want that, originally, but things have changed."

I waited for Leo to tell me he was just kidding, that he wanted to make me feel just as shitty as I made him feel. But Leo wasn't like that. He was honest. Open. More so than I could ever be. But I was trying.

"So what's changed?" Leo asked.

"Do I have to answer that?" I cringed.

"Yes. I deserve some emoting here, and besides, you're adorable when you're all squirmy."

"Fuck you. I'm not adorable." I whacked him in the chest.

"You are until you open your mouth," he decided. "Fess up."

I exhaled a deep sigh. "Fine. But you owe me, like, a foot massage or something for this."

"A foot massage?" he laughed.

"Yeah. Isn't that what couples do for each other?"

"Couples? Are we a couple?"

"You're killing me, Leo." I covered my face with my hand and attempted to spill. "I just realized that it's okay to give and get good things sometimes, and it doesn't make me a bad person if my life isn't one hundred percent hell." There. I said it.

"Aw." He patted my head. "Was that so hard?"

"You'll find out later when I kill you in your sleep."

"I get so turned on when you talk like that." He moved my hand away from my face and kissed me. I couldn't fathom how I found a guy who liked me for my good and evil parts. But there I was, in the arms of Leo Dietz again, and I wasn't hating myself for it.

CHAPTER

39

THAT MONDAY, AS I NAVIGATED the hallway at school, I felt different. The dread was still there when I thought about Becca, the "what if" of the rest of her forever-pending test results. But Becca had returned to the person I knew as my best friend. Not fighting her discomfort anymore, she chose to stay home from school until she was ready. Her mom was more than okay with that, since it went along with her whole doomed vibe. Luckily, her mom spent so much time out of the house it allowed Caleb that much more time in. Becca drew an old-timey picture in my mind of her recuperating in bed while Caleb sat next to her reading love poems and refreshing her mint juleps.

Jenna Brown strode up to my locker as I finagled space for my backpack. "I hear Becca's still sick." She pouted overzealously.

"Her mom tell your mom that?" I was ready to jump down her throat.

She nodded. "The drama department put some money together

to get her this." She handed me a small box with a card attached. "It's an iTunes gift card. So she can download TV shows and movies to keep her busy." Jenna had a slight look of panic as she explained this, as though I would have an abusively snarky comeback. I thought about it, like why it took them so damn long or how would her mom know how she was because she was never around anyway. I stopped myself. What they did was a good thing. I couldn't fault them for taking a while to do it.

"Thanks. I'll give this to her. I'm sure she'll appreciate it."

Jenna stood stock still, waiting for the punch line. I thought about fulfilling her expectations, when we were interrupted by the appearance of a super-tall figure behind her. I looked up at him and smiled. If I were one of those people, my eyes might have welled up with tears.

"Excuse me," Leo said to Jenna, and stepped between her and me.

"Hi," I breathed. He didn't say anything, just leaned down, hands cupping my face, and kissed me. It was my first instance of hallway PDA, something I held so much disdain for I made it a point to mock regular culprits as a sport.

But Leo's lips on my lips, his hands on my cheeks, and I wasn't even in the hallway anymore. It was only me and Leo. Heavenly.

Until Jenna interrupted with a giggle and an overly enthusiastic "Are you guys dating? That is so cute!" She squealed.

"Leo and I are not cute," I blasted her. But what was I really fighting about? I wrapped an arm around his waist, and he draped his over my shoulder. "And, yes, we are dating. Or whatever," I admitted.

"Adorable!" she squealed again. I willed myself not to kick her in the shin.

"We have to go," I announced, and pulled Leo along as best I could through the hall to the book closet. When we arrived, Leo fished out his key and unlocked the door. Inside for the first time in months, Leo looked around. "Something looks different. Did you rearrange the books?" he asked.

"Maybe. Long story," I dismissed. He kissed me again, and I wanted to pull the clocks off the wall to stop time.

Every day of school after that started the exact same way. I had never looked forward to school, or a guy, as much in my life.

I prayed that the third bad thing had come and gone.

CHAPTER

THREE WEEKS PASSED faster than any I could remember before my dad died. For so long, time stood still, dragged, or even moved backward as I focused on every negative, painful thing that happened and wondered what would come next. My guard was only down the tiny bit I allowed myself, as Becca waited for the test results of her cancer treatment. Her radiation was over, and instead of us spending more time together as her health improved, we saw each other less and less. I hated to admit it was because of a guy, but Leo and I were hanging out whenever we could, watching movies, studying at the library, brainstorming a movie I might make someday. Not that Becca wasn't busy with her own guy. Now that she was starting to feel human again, hair growing back, weight filling out her sunken frame, Caleb was in the picture a lot more. They went from romantic notes between windows to sharing her twin bed most nights. I wondered if Becca's mom knew what was going on, considering Caleb was a rather large guy to hide. Maybe she was of the mind that Becca went through hell and deserved her little slice of homeschooled heaven. Or maybe she was too cracked out on God to notice.

Leo and I hung out with Becca and Caleb from time to time. He was nice, mind-blowingly smart, but definitely a little pop-culture deprived. I feel like if I were homeschooled it would be impossible not to waste the day in front of the television or computer and try to pass it off as "homework." But Caleb was all about actual learning. He did deign to come to a midnight screening of *The Exorcist* with us. Leo and I disagreed on its brilliance. "I think there's way too much plot and not enough scare," I argued.

"Which makes the scary parts all the scarier. Plus, there's all that subliminal stuff," Leo countered. We discovered on a Blu-ray of the film that the director did all of these extra-creepy secret things, like inserting random, terrifying faces into scenes and playing the squeals of actual pigs being slaughtered to make the movie especially unsettling.

"I'll take a midnight show of *Casablanca* over this any day," was Caleb's response. Becca stared at him dreamily. It was a good look for her after so many pained ones.

And still we waited for the news of her life.

Becca began making school appearances again, not full days but enough to get some work done. One day at lunch, her phone rang. Becca's cancer was like a get-out-of-jail-free card and allowed her to carry her cell phone in case of emergency. "Emergency" most of the time meant texting sappy *I miss you* texts to Caleb, but it was nearing the time of her lab results. Post-chemo, post-radiation, she'd soon find out if the cancer was zapped, if she needed to go through hell again, or the worst possibility: Treatment didn't work at all.

When her phone rang, Becca announced, "It's my mom," which

it often was. When Becca was the one out of the house, her mom called to check in every hour or so. She admitted to wishing Helen could follow Becca around school so she didn't have to worry so much. I don't think anything could have stopped her mom from worrying. It felt a tad more appropriate than a facial.

"Hello?" Becca stood up and plugged one ear to hear the phone better. The lunch crew followed her expressions. Anticipation. Disappointment. Aggravation.

"Mom! Stop calling me! Seriously. Unless you have news, don't call anymore. You're going to make me have a heart attack before I even find out if my cancer is gone." Pause. "Yeah, love you, too. *Crazy woman*," she mumbled at the end.

The following Saturday morning I was busy slicing cucumbers at Cellar when my phone rang in my pocket. I normally didn't answer it, mostly because then I had to wash my hands for the millionth time. Winter dryness was killing me. But all phone calls had become critical. I knew any day Becca would learn of her post-chemo scans, which would basically say whether her cancer had gone away. Seven months. That's how long I watched Becca have cancer. That's a long fucking time to be sick with anything, to have to watch and wonder what was going to happen to my best friend. Could this finally be the call?

I walked into the back room, away from the kitchen scraps and music from the stereo. "Hello?" I answered.

I played out this phone call a billion times in my head. Sometimes it went:

"I have to tell you something, Alex. The cancer's still there. And it's spread."

And when I'm feeling particularly morbid, Becca adds,

"They say I have one month to live."

I also have the other conversation, where Becca screams at the top of her lungs, "The cancer's gone!!!" We dance, and I hug whoever's closest to me, preferably not some sub-slinging douche.

"Hello?" This wasn't in my head. This was the real deal. The phone call that determined our future. My hands shook as I answered. I hadn't realized how terrified I was.

There was no dramatic pause. Instead, unlike any of my pre-enactments, Becca blurted out, "I'm clear. No cancer spots. Normal blood." She was breathlessly quiet.

"That's good, right? I mean, it sounds good. I just never know if there's something else coming."

"Eighty-five percent full remission rate. That's really good. I go back again in three months. And three months after that." I let the tears of relief tumble down my cheeks.

"That's a lot of waiting," I told her.

"It's not waiting, Alex. It's living. For the next three months, I'm going to live like we're gonna die young!" she screamed.

"That was Ke$ha, wasn't it?" I wiped my eyes with my palm.

"Brilliant woman, she is."

"Doesn't she have the words 'suck it' tattooed inside her lip?" I asked.

"Don't you have a tattoo of a dead guy smiley on your leg?" She got me.

"Brilliant woman, she is," I concurred.

I exhaled at the realization that, indeed, for the next three months there was no more cancer. We could end our senior year like normal teenagers. Or, at the very least, like normal teenagers with a shitload of baggage.

CHAPTER

41

"**DO WE HAVE TO** do this?" I asked, bundled in twelve layers of clothes and still freezing my ass off at Baynes Beach.

"Bucket list, remember?" Becca still held that Fuck-It List over my head, as if the fact that I started it with her made me obligated to finish it, too.

"I believe we decided it was a Fuck-It List, and that is what I'd like to declare right now. Fuck it. It's too cold out, Becca!" Becca used her cancer card to convince me, Caleb, and Leo to fulfill number 13: Sleep on a beach and watch the sunrise.

"I'm calling a technicality. It doesn't actually say we have to stay all night. Let's just watch the sun set and then get up really early for the sunrise." Leo was my glowing voice of reason.

"Yes! Excellent idea." I clapped.

"You guys can leave after sunset. We're staying." Becca linked her arm through Caleb's massive one. He was scouty prepared with a tent, heater, and probably a bearskin rug he skinned himself.

The four of us sat on a blanket in the cold sand. Caleb passed out hot chocolate made from cacao beans he grew in his greenhouse. Probably. As miserable as the late March temperature was, nothing could really make the moment bad. Here we were, together, happy, alive. So little else mattered.

Still, the instant Caleb marked the sunset with his Swiss Army watch, Leo and I were out of there. "Call me if you stop feeling your toes," I yelled from my car. Leo and I sat inside as the engine attempted to warm up.

"Just drive. We'll be back at my house in five minutes. We can warm up there."

In the time Leo and I had been back on speaking terms, closer than when it was merely physical, we hadn't yet had sex. At first, we held out so as not to make things too intense too quickly. But as the weeks passed—the long, yearning, painful weeks—I didn't think I could hold out much longer. It surprised me, that while getting emotionally close to someone I could feel even more attracted to him than when I barely knew anything about him. I knew that sounded stupid, but I had never experienced anything different. The physical and the emotional never went together. Maybe because I had never had the emotional before.

We got back to Leo's house in record time and shot straight up to his bedroom. We kicked off our shoes and dove under the covers together, still wearing all eight million layers of clothing. As we huddled up, our shivers stopped and we somehow fell asleep. When I awoke an hour later, I was thick with sweat.

"Gross." I sat up and began to peel off my coat, then my hoodie. Underneath were three more shirts and long underwear. When all that was left was my t-shirt, I nudged Leo awake. His forehead and hairline were coated in sweat. "You need to get out of your clothes," I told him.

"Yes, ma'am," he said sleepily. I helped him unzip his coat and pulled layer after layer over his head. When it was time to stop, when he, too, was left with only a black t-shirt, I pulled that off, too. In return, he yanked my shirt over my head. "Just to be fair," he explained.

"Well, if you're going to be that way," I said, and unhooked my bra.

There we were on his bed, wearing jeans and nothing else. I sat on my knees facing him, while his legs dangled over the edge of the bed. I traced my fingers up the definition of his stomach, his chest. He wrapped his hands around my waist and let them rise up over my breasts. This was as naked as we'd been in months. We both knew that if any clothing came off, we couldn't stop ourselves from everything coming off. We were right. The instant I felt his bare flesh against mine, I couldn't get close enough to him.

We took our time, knowing we *had* time. Every hair on my body stood on end, every sense heightened. He tasted so good, felt even better. I didn't remember taking off my jeans, and maybe I didn't. Maybe it was all him. We waited until we couldn't stand it anymore, until it felt like we'd explode from not letting ourselves go. And then we did. The feeling lasted forever, as though I couldn't let it stop. When I finally relaxed, every limb entwined with Leo, I said something so completely involuntary that I gasped after I said it.

"I love you."

"You what?" Leo propped himself up on an elbow.

"Uhhh . . ." I sounded like a dolt, and I knew I had to own it. "I said I love you," I repeated more clearly, more certain.

"One more time," Leo prodded.

"Those are about to be the last words you ever hear, Leo Dietz," I growled in his ear.

"That'd be fine with me." He kissed my forehead. I waited for his return sentiment, but it didn't come.

"And?" I prodded.

"And what?" He played dumb. Or *was* dumb.

"Aren't you going to say it back?"

"You heard those words from me and had months to deal with them. I'm going to let your words age a little. Like a fine wine."

"Or cheese," I noted.

"I like cheese," Leo added. "A lot."

"That makes two of us," I concurred.

So, I had to wait. I had gotten pretty good at waiting. But this time, it wasn't test results. Love was so abstract: It wasn't war, it wasn't cancer, it wasn't death. But I'm pretty sure that's what I felt. And I was going to let myself, no matter how hard my evil side fought against it.

CHAPTER

SPRING

I WAITED FOR LEO in the book closet. There was less than one month left of school. Less than one month until the anniversary of my dad's death. Less than one month until Becca's next cancer check.

The door clicked open, and there stood Leo. His hair was growing out, which I liked a little better than the buzz. I think we all wanted to have some hair on our heads for a while. He had on a black t-shirt, jeans, and black Chucks, which made us annoyingly cutesy and matching. I recognized the outline of his brother's dog tags underneath his shirt. The second he walked in and the door closed, we clung to each other. We kissed for a couple minutes until I stopped him. "Time to get down to business."

Reluctantly, we sat down at the old desks and worked. He had a huge creative writing story to revise, and I was putting the finishing touches on my new horror movie, *Graphite*. It was the story of a girl who gets hit in the forehead with a pencil after her classmates attempt to throw it at the muddled classroom celling. Then she goes on a killing spree, taking out all of the guys who crossed her with violent pencil deaths. Naturally, Becca would star, fulfilling number nineteen on the Fuck-It List. Not that we had looked at the list since freezing our asses off on the beach. We may have accomplished most of the weird, ridiculous, perverted goals Becca set for herself, but the list felt too connected to cancer to continue. I held onto it, storing it underneath my bedside stack of library books. Just in case. Becca never asked where it was.

On a clear May afternoon, Becca, Caleb, Leo, and I hung out in Becca's backyard. It was the spring of the seventeen-year cicadas. They had been around when I was a baby, so this was technically the first time I had really seen them. I found them fascinating. In appearance, they would have made perfect horror-movie specimens: about three inches long, with translucent, green wings and glowing red eyes. Their feet were covered with sticky pads, and if one landed on you it might stay and just hang out, not flit away like scaredy bugs. It was incredible to think they lay dormant underground for seventeen years. Then they climbed their way out, leaving behind a trail of cocoony things on the trees and a layer of bugs on the ground so thick you had to shuffle your way through them so you wouldn't crush their newly freed bodies. And the noise they made was deafening. Like a UFO landed somewhere nearby and hovered as it picked up people for experiments.

There definitely was a movie or two to be made out of this.

Caleb's beagle waddled around, his belly distended after consuming more than his share of the tasty bugs, three of which rested on my arm. I examined them, and asked, "Do you think they dreamed?"

"Hmmm?" Becca mused as she rested her head on Caleb's lap, and he stroked her newly growing hair.

"For seventeen years. Do you think they dreamed underground for seventeen years?" I clarified.

"Do any bugs dream?" Caleb asked.

"It's so sad. To wake up and die so soon after," Becca said.

"I bet it's really fucking awesome for those couple of weeks when they're awake, though," Leo noted.

"Maybe they spend seventeen years dreaming about what they want to do during their minuscule lives." I smiled at the thought of bug dreams. Then something came to me. "Hey, Becca. I wonder if they have bucket lists."

"A bug-it list!" She laughed.

"That was so not funny," I said. "Okay. Maybe a little."

I shook my arm, and the three bugs lazily flew away, on their way to accomplish great things in a short amount of time. Really, how we all should try to live our lives. No matter how long we've got.

Becca's
FUCK-~~Bucket~~-IT List

1. Have a Kool-Aid stand with every Kool-Aid flavor invented.
2. Stick my tongue to a frozen pole.
3. Chew 10 pieces of gum at once and blow a quadruple bubble.
4. ~~Write Rupert Grint a love letter~~
5. Wear two different shoes.
6. Send my bra to Zac Efron.
7. Eat a hot pepper.
8. Crank call Adam Levitz.
9. Bake cookies for the janitor.
10. Hop a train like a hobo.
11. MASTURBATE.
12. Kiss a boy who smokes
13. Sleep on a beach and watch the sunrise.
14. ~~Tell off Lottie McDaniels~~
15. FLASH THE HOMESCHOOL BOY NEXT DOOR.
16. Smoke pot with a burnout behind the school.
17. Make out with a burnout behind the school.
18. Have sex with a football stud, and dump him the next day.
19. Star in one of Alex's movies, and have it seen by actual people instead of just me and Alex.
20. Go to school dressed like a prostitute.
21. Touch Jamie Bamber's butt.
22. Take a bath in someone else's house.
23. Have sex with someone I'm in love with and who's in love with me.

ACKNOWLEDGMENTS

Cylon Basestar–sized thanks go out to the following people:

Allyx Davison, for letting me into your life and showing me I need to upgrade my video game knowledge.

Becky Britt, for introducing me to Allyx, and your sincerity and thoughts.

Dale Davison, for the online time line of Allyx's treatment on CaringBridge.com. It was more helpful than any book or Web site in keeping my character's journey on track.

Eastman, Jack, and Al, for always answering my questions.

Jean, for the wonderful bucket list spark; Anna, for the lengthy editorial phone fun; Liz, for her glorious editorial prowess; Rich, April, Dave, Ksenia, and all of the other wonderful people at my publisher, Feiwel and Friends; and my agent, Rosemary Stimola, for her guidance and pumpkins.

My mom, for all of her support, love, and being the best grandma ever.

And Matt and Romy, who start each day with a hilarious, human alarm clock and end each day with snuggles and songs. Thank you for holding me up when way too many chips are down.

QUESTIONS FOR THE AUTHOR

JULIE HALPERN

What did you want to be when you grew up?
I don't think I knew as a kid. In junior high, we had to do a presentation on a profession, something we might want to be, but part of the project was to interview someone. I was too shy to find someone in an actual field of interest, so I interviewed my mom's friend, an accountant. I think I went with that for one or two more career assignments. At the end of high school, I wanted to go into film, which was one of my college majors. But after interning on *The Adventures of Pete & Pete* and having a total blast, I realized the business side of it wasn't for me. I eventually ended up with a master's degree in Library and Information Science and was a school librarian for ten years before I left to write and stay home with my children. I may go back to being a librarian someday. It was really fun.

What were your hobbies as a kid? What are your hobbies now?
Is watching TV a hobby? I watched way too much TV as a kid. My childhood was when home computers were just starting to take off, so I really got into our Apple 2GS. I made banners

and newspapers and played "Where in the World Is Carmen Sandiego?" Now? I still like computer games, although as a parent, it's pretty much impossible to find the time to play them. And I like to plan vacations, even if I have no money to take them.

How did you celebrate publishing your first book?
I don't remember what happened when *Get Well Soon* came out, but I do remember when I talked to my editor while I was at work, and she told me they wanted to acquire my book. I ran out from my office into the school library and said, "My book is going to be published!" There were two kids in the library, and they appeased me with the slow clap. Very triumphant.

Where do you write your books?
At this point, wherever I can. I can't write with any noise, so I try to book a private room at the public library when I have a deadline. But most days, I'm too busy with my kids to do that, so I will write with earplugs in. I wrote half of *The F- It List* while sitting in the car while my daughter was in preschool.

Who was your favorite teacher in high school?
I had an English teacher who ran a philosophy club, which I thought was cool. He took the club to a horror movie conference at a neighboring high school, and that kind of changed my life in terms of film knowledge. I also had a gym teacher I really liked; he never made me feel bad for being an out-of-shape runner. Plus, he had this ridiculous routine where he'd play Hulk Hogan's theme song to get us pumped up before a run. I wish I had included that in the book!

What's your idea of fun?
I like going places—museums, comic book conventions, Renaissance fairs, jelly bean factories (all places I go on a regular basis)—with my family.

What's your favorite song?
"The Door into Summer" by the Monkees.

Who is your favorite fictional character?
Buffy Summers from *Buffy the Vampire Slayer*.

What was your favorite book when you were a kid? Do you have a favorite book now?
Mouse Tales by Arnold Lobel. It is still my favorite book. ". . . And what nice new feet you have." Could there be anything better?

What's your favorite TV show?
Of all time, it would be the original Degrassi series from the late 80s/90s, *Buffy the Vampire Slayer*, *Beverly Hills 90210* (also the original), and *Battlestar Galactica* (the newer version). Currently, I'm really into *Supernatural*.

If you could travel anywhere in the world, where would you go and what would you do?
I would go back to Australia, with my family this time. I lived there and traveled all around after college, and I learned so much. I felt a real connection to the red earth, the animals, the people, the history, and even the spiders. They have A LOT of spiders.

If you could travel in time, where would you go and what would you do?
I would go to the 1893 World's Columbian Exposition in Chicago. That makes me sound much more old-fashioned than I actually am, but something about the wonder and the newness of so many things, especially in my beloved hometown, has always seemed really magical to me.

What advice do you wish someone had given you when you were younger?
I don't know if I would have listened to anyone's advice when I was younger, so it probably wouldn't have mattered if they gave it to me.

Do you ever get writer's block? What do you do to get back on track?
I don't. Not that everything I write is easy and stellar, but I just try to write anything—even if it's the character going to the bathroom. At least I'm moving the story along, among other things. . . .

If you were a superhero, what would your superpower be?
Flight. Airplane rides can be pretty excruciating.

What do you wish you could do better?
Break-dance.

What do you want readers to remember about your books?
Everybody is weird in some way.

WHAT ROAD TRIP WOULD BE COMPLETE WITHOUT A LITTLE FRIENDSHIP, ADVENTURE, AND A FAKE KIDNAPPING?

READ MORE FOR A SNEAK PEEK AT

CHAPTER ONE

I did it," Penny's voice whispers on my voicemail. Confused, I push the button to replay. "I did it." That's all she said. According to Robot Phone Woman Time Keeper, Penny called at exactly 4:47 a.m., a rather unacceptable time to call anyone on a Saturday morning, and most certainly not on the Saturday morning after the Friday that was our last day of high school EVER. Because it is the first Saturday of the rest of our lives, finally past all of the clique clack crud of high school, I allow myself to sleep past my mother's acceptable sleep hour of exactly 11:59 ("At least it's still morning") until 1:43 in the afternoon. Which makes me approximately nine hours too late to stop Penny.

How did it become my responsibility to help this pathetic soul anyway? We weren't ever friends until this past year, and even then only by default. I had no choice really, unless I wanted to be a total hag by not asking her to join us at the Lunch Table of Misfit Toys, dubbed so by our paltry group of seniors in lunch period 8, who were so placed because we chose not to stress ourselves out with AP classes, resulting in a more pliable schedule for the admin to have their way with. Instead of the race for the maximum number of AP credits possible, I selected some easy, breezy independent studies of things I actually enjoy doing, like Creative Writing and Photo. Why bother with the AP BS anyway? So you can graduate college early? No thanks. I breezed through my senior year like I plan to breeze through this summer, living off the fat of the land that is my bat mitzvah savings, and just chilling out. No worries. Or at least, that was the plan.

"I did it." Who leaves a message like that? Who is so paranoid that they have to be so cryptic? If this wasn't day one of my Summer of Nothing, I might be in a hurry to figure this out. But first: breakfast. Or lunch, really. Snack? Lack, or lunk maybe. It is a bowl of cereal, whatever it is. I like to fancy myself a cereal connoisseur. Today, slightly out of it and in need of substance *and* energy, I mix some Frosted Mini-Wheats with Cookie Crisp, and throw in a few Craisins for fruit and texture. I shake up the skim milk, splash it on, toss around the cereal pieces with a spoon to make sure each piece is coated with milk, and plant myself in front of the computer. Then I second-guess it. Maybe I don't want my lunk interrupted by the possibility of more Penny drivel waiting on the other side of the screen, so I flip on the TV instead. An actual video is on

MTV. Hip-hop or rap or something. Not my scene. But I can't help wishing I had a butt like that girl in the video. I wonder how she buys jeans, though.

"I did it." It's like Penny's voice is floating out of my cereal from between the flakes and the crisps. How did she say it? It wasn't urgent or terrified, like someone calling 911 from under her bed as she waits for a killer to enter her room, nor was it excited or light or distracted or a million other adjectives I can think of. She just sounded flat, like the only reason she left the message at all was to keep a record of her existence.

Before I call Penny, you know, just to clarify things, I decide to call my best friend, Josh. Although, if there's one person who can outsleep me, it's him, and I say this from experience. Sadly the experience is due to the fact that he and I are so platonic that his dad and my mom could give a rat turd if I sleep at his house or he sleeps at mine. On the couch, of course. So damn pathetic, then, that I am so madly in love with him. Cliché, touché, but true. I've spent four years waiting for something to happen between us that is more than just sharing a toothbrush when he forgets to bring his own. This summer is the last chance, before I head off to college and he heads off to tour Europe with his band or records the Next Big Thing album he always talks about or possibly moves to Saskatoon to hunt moose. He doesn't know where he'll go, but it sure isn't college. And it's most definitely not in any way, shape, or form dependent on anything I do or anywhere I go. But, damn, I wish it was.

I decide to try and wake him. The phone only rings twice before Josh picks up.

"Heeeyyyy." He sounds awake and happy to see me on the caller ID, which gives my stomach a buzz. I remember once at school when I was talking to some randomer, and Josh came out of the bathroom, me not expecting to see him there because he had Español at the time, and this randomer, upon seeing the two of us see each other, said, "It's like you guys haven't seen each other in weeks. That's how happy you look." And I thought, *Him, too?*

"Good afternoon, sir. May I interest you in a pointless quest?" Josh and I like to go for long walks or drives with fake purposes and dub them quests. Once we spent an entire afternoon "looking for love in all the wrong places," like that super-lame old country song. We looked under rocks, at Ben & Jerry's, in the sand box at Stroger Park. I thought maybe, just maybe, he'd get the hint that love was standing right next to him in a cute pair of cut-offs, but Josh seemed to miss that somehow.

"I'll meet you at Stroger in twenty. And I hope you don't mind, but I have evening stink." Josh isn't much of a fan of showering on a regular basis, which may put off some, but I prefer his sleep smell to some covered-up soap smell any day.

I finish my cereal, drop the bowl in the sink, and tug on a blue bra, blue T-shirt, and jean shorts. Some days I like to be monochromed, just for the hell of it. I brush my teeth, tug my chin-length golden brown hair into a nub of a ponytail, shuffle my way into a pair of flip-flops, and I'm out the door.

The air smells free. Free from class schedules and guidance counselors and hallway politics. High school hell is over.

"I did it." Damn that message. Damn Penny for glomming her way into my life. I wish I didn't care. It's messing with my new freedom vibe.

Three blocks away is Stroger Park, big when I was little and little now that I'm, well, big. Two regular swings, a tire swing, two baby swings, a slide, a wall climb, some monkey bars, and plenty of woodchips to stick in your flip-flops. I always wondered, *Why the woodchips?* It seemed like there would be more woodchip-in-the-eye accidents than woodchips-as-saviors-for-falling-children incidents. Or maybe I just missed them because I was too busy, you know, being a kid.

Josh hangs upside down from the monkey bars, shirtless (as is his summer look), his self-cut, shoulder-length brown hair dangling below him. I try not to ogle, but, damn, he looks amazing without a shirt. How do guys get to look so good without exercising or eating well at all? He's skinny, but not too skinny, and all nice and defined. I exhale a platonic sigh.

"Hey, Lil," he calls and swings himself off the bars, stumbling onto the woodchips. Even graceless, he's gorgeous. "You smell that?" he asks as I approach him, and I sit down on the metal ladder to the monkey bars.

"Well, what do you expect when you don't shower?" I ask.

"No." He chuckles in his slow, slack way. He grabs the high bar closest to me and hangs himself so he can easily kick my knees with his ratty black Chucks. "Not me." He takes a huge sniff of air. "*That*. That smell. The rest of our lives." He grins big and I grin bigger. Our lives are going somewhere away from here. *Like Penny*, I remember.

"I got a message. This morning. From Penny."

"Poor little lamb." Josh always teases me about Penny because I befriended her out of pity, but he plays along, too. We're both too nice to let her go it alone. "What'd she say?" he asks me, still hanging.

I ignore the shoes on my knees. "'I did it.'" I look up at him and whisper it the same way she whispered to my voicemail.

"Did what?" he asks, but not curious enough. "*It?*" He laughs, although we both know she did *it* a long time ago, thanks to the pregnancy scare aftermath I had to clean up.

"She told me she was going to do something the other